Derek Mahon

SELECTED POEMS

VIKING/GALLERY
in association with
OXFORD UNIVERSITY PRESS

VIKING

Published by the Penguin Group
27 Wrights Lane, London w8 5tz, England
Penguin Books USA Inc., 375 Hudson Street, New York, New York 10014, USA
Penguin Books Australia Ltd, Ringwood, Victoria, Australia
Penguin Books Canada Ltd, 10 Alcorn Avenue, Toronto, Ontario, Canada m4v 3b2
Penguin Books (NZ) Ltd, 182–190 Wairau Road, Auckland 10, New Zealand

Penguin Books Ltd, Registered Offices: Harmondsworth, Middlesex, England

GALLERY

The Gallery Press, Loughcrew, Oldcastle, County Meath, Ireland

This collection first published in Great Britain by Viking and in Ireland
by The Gallery Press in association with Oxford University Press 1991
5 7 9 10 8 6 4

The Gallery Press acknowledge the assistance of
An Chomhairle Ealaíon/The Arts Council, Ireland

Photoset in Garamond by Redsetter Ltd, in Dublin, designed by
Peter Fallon and originated in Ireland

Printed in Great Britain by Butler & Tanner Ltd, Frome and London

A CIP catalogue record for this book is available from the British Library

ISBN 0 670 83575 7 VIKING
ISBN 1 85235 062 8 GALLERY

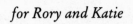

for Rory and Katie

Contents

In Carrowdore Churchyard

(at the grave of Louis MacNeice)

Your ashes will not stir, even on this high ground,
However the wind tugs, the headstones shake.
This plot is consecrated, for your sake,
To what lies in the future tense. You lie
Past tension now, and spring is coming round
Igniting flowers on the peninsula.

Your ashes will not fly, however the rough winds burst
Through the wild brambles and the reticent trees.
All we may ask of you we have; the rest
Is not for publication, will not be heard.
Maguire, I believe, suggested a blackbird
And over your grave a phrase from Euripides.

Which suits you down to the ground, like this churchyard
With its play of shadow, its humane perspective.
Locked in the winter's fist, these hills are hard
As nails, yet soft and feminine in their turn
When fingers open and the hedges burn.
This, you implied, is how we ought to live —

The ironical, loving crush of roses against snow,
Each fragile, solving ambiguity. So
From the pneumonia of the ditch, from the ague
Of the blind poet and the bombed-out town you bring
The all-clear to the empty holes of spring,
Rinsing the choked mud, keeping the colours new.

Glengormley

Wonders are many and none is more wonderful than man
Who has tamed the terrier, trimmed the hedge
And grasped the principle of the watering can.
Clothes-pegs litter the window-ledge
And the long ships lie in clover; washing lines
Shake out white linen over the chalk thanes.

Now we are safe from monsters, and the giants
Who tore up sods twelve miles by six
And hurled them out to sea to become islands
Can worry us no more. The sticks
And stones that once broke bones will not now harm
A generation of such sense and charm.

Only words hurt us now. No saint or hero,
Landing at night from the conspiring seas,
Brings dangerous tokens to the new era —
Their sad names linger in the histories.
The unreconciled, in their metaphysical pain,
Dangle from lamp-posts in the dawn rain;

And much dies with them. I should rather praise
A worldly time under this worldly sky —
The terrier-taming, garden-watering days
Those heroes pictured as they struggled through
The quick noose of their finite being. By
Necessity, if not choice, I live here too.

Grandfather

They brought him in on a stretcher from the world,
Wounded but humorous; and he soon recovered.
Boiler-rooms, row upon row of gantries rolled
Away to reveal the landscape of a childhood
Only he can recapture. Even on cold
Mornings he is up at six with a block of wood
Or a box of nails, discreetly up to no good
Or banging round the house like a four-year-old —

Never there when you call. But after dark
You hear his great boots thumping in the hall
And in he comes, as cute as they come. Each night
His shrewd eyes bolt the door and set the clock
Against the future, then his light goes out.
Nothing escapes him; he escapes us all.

Preface to a Love Poem

This is a circling of itself and you —
A form of words, compact and compromise,
   Prepared in the false dawn of the half-true
Beyond which the shapes of truth materialize.
   This is a blind with sunlight filtering through.

   This is a stirring in the silent hours,
As lovers do with thoughts they cannot frame
   Or leave, but bring to darkness like night-flowers,
Words never choosing but the words choose them —
   Birds crowing, wind whistling off pale stars.

   This is a night-cry, neither here nor there,
A ghostly echo from the clamorous dead
   Who cried aloud in anger and despair
Outlasting stone and bronze, but took instead
   Their lost grins underground with them for ever.

   This is at one remove, a substitute
For final answers; but the wise man knows
   To cleave to the one living absolute
Beyond paraphrase, and shun a shrewd repose.
   The words are aching in their own pursuit

   To say 'I love you' out of indolence
As one might speak at sea without forethought,
   Drifting inconsequently among islands.
This is a way of airing my distraught
   Love of your silence; you are the soul of silence.

De Quincey in Later Life

Tonight the blessèd state, that long repose
Where time is measured
Not by the clock but by the hours
Of the wind; his seventh heaven when it snows
The valley under, and the frosty stars
Sing to his literary leisure.

Hearth rugs, a tea-pot and a quart
Decanter of laudanum —
Perihelion of paradise! No sort
Or condition of men but is the less human
For want of this. *Mens sana*
In corpore sano.

Excellent as an antidote for toothache
And the busy streets. Wood crackles better
In a head removed, and fresh water
Springs wiselier in a heart that isn't sick.
And then the Piranesi dreams came, and his children
Woke him every day at noon —

Until he cried out, 'I shall sleep no more!',
And quit the hot sheets and the enormous
Apparitions dying on the floor.
He left the house,
Walked out to the sunlight on the hill
And heard, in the whispering-gallery of his soul,

His own small, urgent discord echoing back
From dark roads taken at random
And the restless thunder of London —
Where he had gone in his eighteenth year
And walked the embankments after dark
With Anne, looking for some such panacea.

Four Walks in the Country Near Saint-Brieuc

1. Morning

No doubt the creation was something like this —
A cold day breaking on silent stones,
Slower than time, spectacular only in size.
First there is darkness, then somehow light;
We call this day, and the other night,
And watch in vain for the second of sunrise.

Suddenly, near at hand, the click of a wooden shoe —
An old woman among the primaeval shapes
Abroad in the field of light, sombrely dressed.
She calls good-day, since there are bad days too,
And her eyes go down. She has seen perhaps
Ten thousand dawns like this, and is not impressed.

2. Man and Bird

All fly away at my approach
As they have done time out of mind,
And hide in the thicker leaves to watch
The shadowy ingress of mankind.

My whistle-talk fails to disarm
Presuppositions of ill-will;
Although they rarely come to harm
The ancient fear is in them still.

Which irritates my *amour propre*
As an enlightened alien
And renders yet more wide the gap
From their world to the world of men.

So perhaps they have something after all —
Either we shoot them out of hand
Or parody them with a bird-call
Neither of us can understand.

3. *After Midnight*
They are all round me in the dark
With claw-knives for my sleepy anarch —

Beasts of the field, birds of the air,
Their slit-eyes glittering everywhere.

I am man self-made, self-made man,
No small-talk now for those who ran

In and out of my muddy childhood.
We have grown up as best we could.

4. *Exit Molloy*
Now at the end I smell the smells of spring
Where in a dark ditch I lie wintering,
And the little town only a mile away
Happy and fatuous in the light of day.
A bell tolls gently; I should start to cry
But my eyes are closed and my face dry.
I am not important and I have to die.
Strictly speaking I am already dead
But still I can hear the birds sing on over my head.

The Forger

When I sold my fake Vermeers to Goering
Nobody knew, nobody guessed
The agony, the fanaticism
Of working beyond criticism
And better than the best.

When they hauled me before the war-crimes tribunal
No-one suspected, nobody knew
The agony of regrets
With which I told my secrets.
They missed the point, of course —
To hell with the national heritage,
I sold my *soul* for potage.

The experts were good value, though,
When they went to work on my studio.
Not I, but *they* were the frauds;
I revolutionized their methods.

Now, nothing but claptrap
About 'mere technique' and 'true vision',
As if there were a distinction —
Their way of playing it down.
But my genius will live on;
For even at one remove
The thing I meant was love.

And I too have wondered
In the dark streets of Holland
With hunger at my belly
When the mists rolled in from the sea;

And I too have suffered
Obscurity and derision,
And sheltered in my heart of hearts
A light to transform the world.

A Portrait of the Artist

(*for Colin Middleton*)

Shivering in the darkness
Of pits, slag-heaps, beetroot fields,
I gasp for light and life
Like a caged bird in spring-time
Banging the bright bars.

Like a glow-worm I move among
The caged Belgian miners,
And the light on my forehead
Is the dying light of faith.
God gutters down to metaphor —

A subterranean tapping, light
Refracted in a glass of beer
As if through a church window,
Or a basin ringed with coal-dust
After the ritual evening bath.

Theo, I am discharged for being
Over-zealous, they call it,
And not dressing the part.
In time I shall go south
And paint what I have seen —

A meteor of golden light
On chairs, faces and old boots,
Setting fierce fire to the eyes
Of sun-flowers and fishing boats,
Each one a miner in disguise.

Day Trip to Donegal

We reached the sea in early afternoon,
Climbed stiffly out. There were things to be done,
Clothes to be picked up, friends to be seen.
As ever, the nearby hills were a deeper green
Than anywhere in the world, and the grave
Grey of the sea the grimmer in that enclave.

Down at the pier the boats gave up their catch,
A writhing glimmer of fish. They fetch
Ten times as much in the city as here,
And still the fish come in year after year —
Herring and mackerel, flopping about the deck
In attitudes of agony and heartbreak.

We left at eight, drove back the way we came,
The sea receding down each muddy lane.
Around midnight we changed-down into suburbs
Sunk in a sleep no gale-force wind disturbs.
The time of year had left its mark
On frosty pavements glistening in the dark.

Give me a ring, goodnight, and so to bed . . .
That night the slow sea washed against my head,
Performing its immeasurable erosions —
Spilling into the skull, marbling the stones
That spine the very harbour wall,
Muttering its threat to villages of landfall.

At dawn I was alone far out at sea
Without skill or reassurance — nobody
To show me how, no promise of rescue —
Cursing my constant failure to take due
Forethought for this; contriving vain
Overtures to the vindictive wind and rain.

An Unborn Child

(for Michael and Edna Longley)

I have already come to the verge of
Departure. A month or so and
I shall be vacating this familiar room.
Its fabric fits me almost like a glove
While leaving latitude for a free hand.
I begin to put on the manners of the world,
Sensing the splitting light above
My head, where in the silence I lie curled.

Certain mysteries are relayed to me
Through the dark network of my mother's body
While she sits sewing the white shrouds
Of my apotheosis. I know the twisted
Kitten that lies there sunning itself
Under the bare bulb, the clouds
Of goldfish mooning around upon the shelf.
In me these data are already vested;

I know them in my bones — bones which embrace
Nothing, for I am completely egocentric.
The pandemonium of encumbrances
Which will absorb me, mind and senses,
Intricacies of the maze and the rat-race,
I imagine only. Though they linger and,
Like fingers, stretch until the knuckles crack,
They cannot dwarf the dimensions of my hand.

I must compose myself at the nerve centre
Of this metropolis, and not fidget —
Although sometimes at night, when the city
Has gone to sleep, I keep in touch with it,
Listening to the warm red water
Running in the sewers of my mother's body;

Or the moths, soft as eyelids, or the rain
Wiping its wet wings on the window-pane:

And sometimes too, in the small hours of the morning
When the dead filament has ceased to ring,
After the goldfish are dissolved in darkness
And the kitten has gathered itself up into a ball
Between the groceries and the sewing,
I slip the trappings of my harness
To range these hollows in discreet rehearsal
And, battering at the concavity of my caul,

Produce in my mouth the words, 'I want to live!' —
This my first protest, and shall be my last.
As I am innocent, everything I do
Or say is couched in the affirmative.
I want to see, hear, touch and taste
These things with which I am to be encumbered.
Perhaps I needn't worry; give
Or take a day or two, my days are numbered.

Canadian Pacific

From famine, pestilence and persecution
Those gaunt forefathers shipped abroad to find
Rough stone of heaven beyond the western ocean,
And staked their claim, and pinned their faith.
Tonight their children whistle through the dark.
Frost chokes the windows; they will not have heard
The wild geese flying south over the lakes
While the lakes harden beyond grief and anger —
The eyes fanatical, rigid the soft necks,
The great wings sighing with a nameless hunger.

Thinking of Inis Oírr in Cambridge, Mass.

(*for Eamon Grennan*)

A dream of limestone in sea-light
Where gulls have placed their perfect prints.
Reflection in that final sky
Shames vision into simple sight;
Into pure sense, experience.
Atlantic leagues away tonight,
Conceived beyond such innocence,
I clutch the memory still, and I
Have measured everything with it since.

Homecoming

Has bath and shave,
clean shirt etc.,
full of potatoes,
rested, yet
badly distraught
by six-hour flight
(Boston to Dublin)
drunk all night
with crashing bore
from Houston, Tex.,
who spoke at length
of guns and sex.
Bus into town
and, sad to say,
no change from when
he went away
two years ago.
Goes into bar,
affixes gaze
on evening star.
Skies change but not
souls change; behold
this is the way
the world grows old.
Scientists, birds,
we cannot start
at this late date
with a pure heart,
or having seen
the pictures plain
be ever innocent again.

A Dying Art

'That day would skin a fairy —
A dying art,' she said.
Not many left of the old trade.
Redundant and remote, they age
Gracefully in dark corners
With lamp-lighters, sail-makers
And native Manx speakers.

And the bone-handled knives with which
They earned their bread? My granny grinds
Her plug tobacco with one to this day.

Ecclesiastes

God, you could grow to love it, God-fearing, God-
    chosen purist little puritan that,
for all your wiles and smiles, you are (the
    dank churches, the empty streets,
the shipyard silence, the tied-up swings) and
    shelter your cold heart from the heat
of the world, from woman-inquisition, from the
    bright eyes of children. Yes you could
wear black, drink water, nourish a fierce zeal
    with locusts and wild honey, and not
feel called upon to understand and forgive
    but only to speak with a bleak
afflatus, and love the January rains when they
    darken the dark doors and sink hard
into the Antrim hills, the bog meadows, the heaped
    graves of your fathers. Bury that red
bandana, stick and guitar; this is your
    country, close one eye and be king.
Your people await you, their heavy washing
    flaps for you in the housing estates —
a credulous people. God, you could do it, God
    help you, stand on a corner stiff
with rhetoric, promising nothing under the sun.

After the Titanic

They said I got away in a boat
And humbled me at the inquiry. I tell you
   I sank as far that night as any
Hero. As I sat shivering on the dark water
   I turned to ice to hear my costly
Life go thundering down in a pandemonium of
   Prams, pianos, sideboards, winches,
Boilers bursting and shredded ragtime. Now I hide
   In a lonely house behind the sea
Where the tide leaves broken toys and hat-boxes
   Silently at my door. The showers of
April, flowers of May mean nothing to me, nor the
   Late light of June, when my gardener
Describes to strangers how the old man stays in bed
   On seaward mornings after nights of
Wind, takes his cocaine and will see no-one. Then it is
   I drown again with all those dim
Lost faces I never understood. My poor soul
   Screams out in the starlight, heart
Breaks loose and rolls down like a stone.
   Include me in your lamentations.

The Studio

You would think with so much going on outside
The deal table would make for the window,
The ranged crockery freak and wail
Remembering its dark origins, the frail
Oil-cloth, in a fury of recognitions,
Disperse in a thousand directions,
And the simple bulb in the ceiling, honed
By death to a worm of pain, to a hair
Of heat, to a light snow-flake laid
On a dark river at night — and wearied
Above all by the life-price of time
And the failure by only a few tenths
Of an inch but completely and for ever
Of the ends of a carefully drawn equator
To meet, sing and be one — abruptly
Roar into the floor.
                    But it
Never happens like that. Instead
There is this quivering silence
In which, day by day, the play
Of light and shadow (shadow mostly)
Repeats itself, though never exactly.

This is the all-purpose bed-, work- and bedroom.
Its mourning faces are cracked porcelain only quicker,
Its knuckles door-knobs only lighter,
Its occasional cries of despair
A function of the furniture.

Aran

(*for Tom Mac Intyre*)

He is earthed to his girl, one hand fastened
In hers, and with his free hand listens,
An earphone, to his own rendition,
Singing the darkness into the light.
I close the pub door gently and step out
Into the yard, and the song goes out,
And a gull creaks off from the tin roof
Of an out-house, planing over the ocean,
Circling now with a hoarse inchoate
Screaming the boned fields of its vision.
God, that was the way to do it,
Hand-clasping, echo-prolonging poet!

Scorched with a fearful admiration
Walking over the nacreous sand,
I dream myself to that tradition,
Fifty winters off the land —
One hand to an ear for the vibration,
The far wires, the reverberation
Down light-years of the imagination
And, in the other hand, your hand.

The long glow springs from the dark soil, however —
No marsh-light holds a candle to this.
Unearthly still in its white weather
A crack-voiced rock-marauder, scavenger, fierce
Friend to no slant fields or the sea either,
Folds back over the forming waters.

Two Songs

1. *His Song*
Months on, you hold me still;
at dawn, bright-rising, like a hill-
horizon, gentle, kind with rain
and the primroses of April.
I shall never know them again
but still your bright shadow
puts out its shadow, daylight, on
the shadows I lie with now.

2. *Her Song*
A hundred men imagine
love when I drink wine;
and then I begin to think
of your words and mine.
The mountain is silent now
where the snow lies fresh,
and my love like the sloe-
blossom on a blackthorn bush.

A Tolerable Wisdom

You keep the cold from the body, the cold from the mind.
Heartscloth, soulswool, without you there would be
Short shrift for the pale beast in a winter's wind,
Too swift exposure by too harsh a sea.
Cold I have known, its sports-pages adrift
Past frozen dodgems in the amusement park,
One crumpled Gauloise thumbing a late lift
Where Paris flamed on the defining dark.

You've heard the gravel at the window, seen
A lost figure unmanned by closing time.
More honour to you that you took him in,
Fed buns and cocoa, sweetness, the sought dream
Of warmth and light against your listening skin
And rocked him to a tolerable wisdom.

An Image from Beckett

In that instant
There was a sea, far off,
As bright as lettuce,

A northern landscape
And a huddle
Of houses along the shore.

Also, I think, a white
Flicker of gulls
And washing hung to dry —

The poignancy of those
Back yards — and the gravedigger
Putting aside his forceps.

Then the hard boards
And darkness once again.
But in that instant

I was struck by the
Sweetness and light,
The sweetness and light,

Imagining what grave
Cities, what lasting monuments,
Given the time.

They will have buried
My great-grandchildren, and theirs,
Beside me by now

With a subliminal batsqueak
Of reflex lamentation.
Our knuckle bones

Litter the rich earth
Changing, second by second,
To civilizations.

It was good while it lasted,
And if it only lasted
The Biblical span

Required to drop six feet
Through a glitter of wintry light,
There is No-One to blame.

Still, I am haunted
By that landscape,
The soft rush of its winds,

The uprightness of its
Utilities and schoolchildren —
To whom in my will,

This, I have left my will.
I hope they have time,
And light enough, to read it.

Lives

(*for Seamus Heaney*)

First time out
I was a torc of gold
And wept tears of the sun.

That was fun
But they buried me
In the earth two thousand years

Till a labourer
Turned me up with a pick
In eighteen fifty-four

And sold me
For tea and sugar
In Newmarket-on-Fergus.

Once I was an oar
But stuck in the shore
To mark the place of a grave

When the lost ship
Sailed away. I thought
Of Ithaca, but soon decayed.

The time that I liked
Best was when
I was a bump of clay

In a Navaho rug,
Put there to mitigate
The too god-like

Perfection of that
Merely human artifact.
I served my maker well —

He lived long
To be struck down in
Tucson by an electric shock

The night the lights
Went out in Europe
Never to shine again.

So many lives,
So many things to remember!
I was a stone in Tibet,

A tongue of bark
At the heart of Africa
Growing darker and darker . . .

It all seems
A little unreal now,
Now that I am

An anthropologist
With my own
Credit card, dictaphone,

Army-surplus boots
And a whole boatload
Of photographic equipment.

I know too much
To be anything any more;
And if in the distant

Future someone
Thinks he has once been me
As I am today,

Let him revise
His insolent ontology
Or teach himself to pray.

Deaths

Who died nails, key-rings,
Sword hilts and lunulae,
Rose hash, bog-paper
And deciduous forests,
Died again these things,

Rose kites, wolves,
Piranha fish, and bleached
To a white femur
By desert, by dark river,

Fight now for our
Fourth lives with an
Informed, articulate
Fury frightening to the
Unreflecting progenitors

Who crowd our oxygen tents.
What should we fear
Who never lost by dying?
What should we not as,

Gunsmiths, botanists, having
Taken the measure of
Life, death, we comb our
Bright souls for
Whatever the past holds?

As It Should Be

We hunted the mad bastard
Through bog, moorland, rock, to the star-lit west
And gunned him down in a blind yard
Between ten sleeping lorries
And an electricity generator.

Let us hear no idle talk
Of the moon in the Yellow River;
The air blows softer since his departure.

Since his tide-burial during school hours
Our children have known no bad dreams.
Their cries echo lightly along the coast.

This is as it should be.
They will thank us for it when they grow up
To a world with method in it.

A Stone Age Figure Far Below

(*for Bill McCormack*)

Through heaving heather, fallen stones
From the wrecked piles of burial cairns
As they fly in over the moors —
Racing about in cloud shadow,
A stone age figure far below
Wildly gesticulating as if
He sees, at last, a sign of life
Or damns them to hell-fires.

When they come with poles, binoculars, whistles,
Blankets and flasks, they will find him dead —
Unkempt, authentic, furnace-eyed
And dead, and his heavy flint hearth-stones
Littered with dung and animal bones;

Or a local resident out for a walk
In tweeds and a hunting hat. 'You must be
Mad,' he will say, 'to suppose this rock
Could accommodate life indefinitely.
Nobody comes here now but me.'

Consolations of Philosophy

(for Eugene Lambe)

When we start breaking up in the wet darkness
And the rotten boards fall from us, and the ribs
Crack under the constriction of tree-roots
And the seasons slip from the fields unknown to us,

Oh, then there will be the querulous complaining
From citizens who had never dreamt of this —
Who, shaken to the bone in their stout boxes
By the latest bright cars, will not inspect them

And, kept awake by the tremors of new building,
Will not be there to comment. When the broken
Wreath bowls are speckled with rain-water
And the grass grows wild for want of a caretaker,

There will be time to live through in the mind
The lives we might have lived, and get them right;
To lie in silence listening to the wind
Mourn for the living through the livelong night.

Gipsies

I have watched the dark police
rocking your caravans
to wreck the crockery
and wry thoughts of peace
you keep there on waste
ground beside motorways
where the snow lies late
(all this on television)
and am ashamed; fed,
clothed, housed and shamed.
You might be interested
to hear, though, that on
stormy nights our strong
double glazing groans with
foreknowledge of death,
the fridge with a great wound,
and not surprised to know
the fate you have so long
endured is ours also.
The cars are piling up.
I listen to the wind
and file receipts; the heap
of scrap metal in my
garden grows daily.

Beyond Howth Head

(*for Jeremy Lewis*)

The wind that blows these words to you
bangs nightly off the black-and-blue
Atlantic, hammering in its haste
dark doors of the declining west
whose rock-built houses year by year
collapse, whose strong sons disappear
(no homespun cottage industries'
embroidered cloths will patch up these

lost townlands on the crumbling shores
of Europe); shivers the dim stars
in rain-water, and spins a single
garage sign behind the shingle.
Fresh from Long Island or Cape Cod
night music finds the lightning rod
of young girls coming from a dance
(you thumbs a lift and takes your chance)

and shakes the radio-sets that play
from Carraroe to Dublin Bay
where, bored to tears by Telefís,
vox populi vox dei, we reach
with twinkling importunity
for good news on the BBC,
our heliotropic Birnam Wood
reflecting an old gratitude.

What can the elders say to this?
The young must kiss and then must kiss
and so by this declension fall
to write the writing on the wall.

A little learning in a parked
Volkswagen torches down the dark
and soon disperses tired belief
with an empiric *joie de vivre*.

The pros outweigh the cons that glow
from Beckett's bleak reductio —
and who would trade self-knowledge for
a prelapsarian metaphor,
love-play of the ironic conscience
for a prescriptive innocence?
'Lewde libertie', whose midnight work
disturbed the peace of Co. Cork

and fired Kilcolman's windows when
the flower of Ireland looked to Spain,
come back and be with us again!
But take a form that sheds for love
that prim conventual disdain
the world beyond knows nothing of;
and flash, an *aisling*, through the dawn
where Yeats's hill-men still break stone.

The writing on the wall, we know,
elsewhere was written long ago.
We fumble with the matches while
the hebona behind the smile
of grammar gets its brisk forensic
smack in the *realpolitik*
and Denmark's hot iambics pass
to the cool courts of Cambridge, Mass. —

leaving us, Jeremy, to flick
blank pages of an empty book
where exponential futures lie
wide to the runways and the sky;
to spin celestial globes of words
over a foaming pint in Ward's,
bowed victims of our linear thought
(though 'booze is bourgeois, pot is not')

rehearsing for the *fin-de-siècle*
gruff Jeremiads to redirect
lost youth into the knacker's yard
of humanistic self-regard;
to praise what will be taken from us,
the memory of Dylan Thomas,
and sign off with a pounding pen
from Seaford or from Cushendun.

I woke this morning (March) to hear
church bells of Monkstown through the roar
of waves round the Martello tower
and thought of the swan-sons of Lir
when Kemoc rang the Christian bell
to crack a fourth-dimensional
world picture, never known again,
and changed them back from swans to men.

It calls as oddly through the wild
eviscerations of the troubled
waters between us and North Wales
where Lycid's ghost for ever sails
(unbosomings of sea-weed, wrack,
industrial bile, a boot from Blackpool,
contraceptives deftly tied
with best regards from Merseyside)

and tinkles with as blithe a sense
of man's cosmic significance
who wrote his world from broken stone,
installed his Word-God on the throne
and placed, in Co. Clare, a sign:
'Stop here and see the sun go down'.
Meanwhile, for a word's sake, the plastic
bombs go off around Belfast;

from the unquiet Cyclades
a Greek poet consults the skies
where sleepless, cold, computed stars
in random sequence light the bars;
and everywhere the ground is thick
with the dead sparrows rhetoric
demands as fictive sacrifice
to prove its substance in our eyes.

Roaring, its ten-lane highways pitch
their naked bodies in the ditch
where once Molloy, uncycled, heard
thin cries of a surviving bird;
but soon Persephone, re-found
in the cold darkness underground,
will speak to the woodlands in fine rain
and the ocean to Cynthia once again.

Spring lights the country; from a thousand
dusty corners, house by house,
from under beds and vacuum cleaners,
empty calor-gas containers,
bread bins, car seats, crates of stout,
the first flies cry to be let out,
to cruise a kitchen, find a door
and die clean in the open air

whose smokeless clarity distils
a chisel's echo in the hills
as if some Noah, weather-wise,
could read a deluge in clear skies.
But nothing ruffles the wind's breath;
this peace is the sweet peace of death
or *l'outre-tombe*. Make no noise,
the foxes have quit Clonmacnoise.

I too, uncycled, might exchange,
since 'we are changed by what we change',
my forkful of the general mess
for hazel-nuts and water-cress
like one of those old hermits who,
less virtuous than some, withdrew
from the world-circles women make
to a small island in a lake.

Chomēi at Tōyama, his blanket
hemp, his character a rank
not-to-be-trusted river mist,
events in Kyōto all grist
to the mill of a harsh irony,
since we are seen by what we see;
Thoreau like ice among the trees
and Spenser, 'farre from enemies',

might serve as models for a while
but to return in greater style.
Centripetal, the hot world draws
its children in with loving claws
from rock and heather, rain and sleet
with only calor-gas for heat
and spins them at the centre where
they have no time to know despair

but still, like Margaret Fuller, must
'accept the universe' on trust
and offer to a phantom future
blood and bones in forfeiture —
each one, his poor loaf on the sea,
monstrous before posterity,
our afterlives a coming true
of perfect worlds we never knew.

The light that left you streaks the walls
of Georgian houses, pubs, cathedrals,
coasters moored below Butt Bridge
and old men at the water's edge
where Anna Livia, breathing free,
weeps silently into the sea,
her tiny sorrows mingling with
the wandering waters of the earth.

And here I close; for look, across
dark waves where bell-buoys dimly toss,
the Bailey winks beyond Howth Head
and sleep calls from the silent bed;
while the moon drags her kindred stones
among the rocks and the strict bones
of the drowned, and I put out the light
on shadows of the encroaching night.

Afterlives

(*for James Simmons*)

1.
I wake in a dark flat
To the soft roar of the world.
Pigeons neck on the white
Roofs as I draw the curtains
And look out over London
Rain-fresh in the morning light.

This is our element, the bright
Reason on which we rely
For the long-term solutions.
The orators yap, and guns
Go off in a back street;
But the faith does not die

That in our time these things
Will amaze the literate children
In their non-sectarian schools
And the dark places be
Ablaze with love and poetry
When the power of good prevails.

What middle-class twits we are
To imagine for one second
That our privileged ideals
Are divine wisdom, and the dim
Forms that kneel at noon
In the city not ourselves.

2.
I am going home by sea
For the first time in years.
Somebody thumbs a guitar
On the dark deck, while a gull
Dreams at the mast-head,
The moon-splashed waves exult.

At dawn the ship trembles, turns
In a wide arc to back
Shuddering up the grey lough
Past lightship and buoy,
Slipway and dry dock
Where a naked bulb burns;

And I step ashore in a fine rain
To a city so changed
By five years of war
I scarcely recognize
The places I grew up in,
The faces that try to explain.

But the hills are still the same
Grey-blue above Belfast.
Perhaps if I'd stayed behind
And lived it bomb by bomb
I might have grown up at last
And learnt what is meant by home.

Leaves

The prisoners of infinite choice
Have built their house
In a field below the wood
And are at peace.

It is autumn, and dead leaves
On their way to the river
Scratch like birds at the windows
Or tick on the road.

Somewhere there is an afterlife
Of dead leaves,
A stadium filled with an infinite
Rustling and sighing.

Somewhere in the heaven
Of lost futures
The lives we might have lived
Have found their own fulfilment.

Dream Days

'When you stop to consider
The days spent dreaming of a future
And say then, that was my life.'

For the days are long —
From the first milk van
To the last shout in the night,
An eternity. But the weeks go by
Like birds; and the years, the years
Fly past anti-clockwise
Like clock hands in a bar mirror.

Nostalgias

The chair squeaks in a high wind,
Rain falls from its branches;
The kettle yearns for the mountain,
The soap for the sea.
In a tiny stone church
On a desolate headland
A lost tribe is singing 'Abide With Me'.

Father-in-Law

While your widow clatters water into a kettle
You lie at peace in your southern grave —
A sea captain who died at sea, almost.
Lost voyager, what would you think of me,
Husband of your fair daughter but impractical?
You stare from the mantelpiece, a curious ghost
In your peaked cap, as we sit down to tea.
The bungalows still signal to the sea,
Rain wanders the golf-course as in your day,
The river still flows past the distillery
And a watery sun shines on Portballintrae.

I think we would have had a lot in common —
Alcohol and the love of one woman
Certainly; but I failed the eyesight test
When I tried for the Merchant Navy,
And lapsed into this lyric lunacy.
When you lost your balance like Li Po
They found unfinished poems in your sea-chest.

Homage to Malcolm Lowry

For gear your typewriter and an old rugby boot,
The voyage started, clearly, when you were born
That danced those empty bottles. When you set out
On a round-the-cosmos trip with the furious Muse
Or lay sweating on a hotel bed in Vera Cruz,
Did you not think you had left that pool astern
Where a soul might bathe and be clean or slake its drought?
In any case, your deportment in those seas
Was faultless. Lightning-blind, you, tempest-torn
At the poles of our condition, did not confuse
The Gates of Ivory with the Gates of Horn.

The Snow Party

(for Louis Asekoff)

Bashō, coming
To the city of Nagoya,
Is asked to a snow party.

There is a tinkling of china
And tea into china;
There are introductions.

Then everyone
Crowds to the window
To watch the falling snow.

Snow is falling on Nagoya
And farther south
On the tiles of Kyōto.

Eastward, beyond Irago,
It is falling
Like leaves on the cold sea.

Elsewhere they are burning
Witches and heretics
In the boiling squares,

Thousands have died since dawn
In the service
Of barbarous kings;

But there is silence
In the houses of Nagoya
And the hills of Ise.

The Last of the Fire Kings

I want to be
Like the man who descends
At two milk churns

With a bulging
String bag and vanishes
Where the lane turns,

Or the man
Who drops at night
From a moving train

And strikes out over the fields
Where fireflies glow,
Not knowing a word of the language.

Either way, I am
Through with history —
Who lives by the sword

Dies by the sword.
Last of the fire kings, I shall
Break with tradition and

Die by my own hand
Rather than perpetuate
The barbarous cycle.

Five years I have reigned
During which time
I have lain awake each night

And prowled by day
In the sacred grove
For fear of the usurper,

Perfecting my cold dream
Of a place out of time,
A palace of porcelain

Where the frugivorous
Inheritors recline
In their rich fabrics
Far from the sea.

But the fire-loving
People, rightly perhaps,
Will not countenance this,

Demanding that I inhabit,
Like them, a world of
Sirens, bin-lids
And bricked-up windows —

Not to release them
From the ancient curse
But to die their creature and be thankful.

A Refusal to Mourn

He lived in a small farm-house
At the edge of a new estate.
The trim gardens crept
To his door, and car engines
Woke him before dawn
On dark winter mornings.

All day there was silence
In the bright house. The clock
Ticked on the kitchen shelf,
Cinders moved in the grate,
And a warm briar gurgled
When the old man talked to himself;

But the door-bell seldom rang
After the milkman went,
And if a shirt-hanger
Knocked in an open wardrobe
That was a strange event
To be pondered on for hours

While the wind thrashed about
In the back garden, raking
The roof of the hen-house,
And swept clouds and gulls
Eastwards over the lough
With its flap of tiny sails.

Once a week he would visit
An old shipyard crony,
Inching down to the road
And the blue country bus
To sit and watch sun-dappled
Branches whacking the windows

While the long evening shed
Weak light in his empty house,
On the photographs of his dead
Wife and their six children
And the Missions to Seamen angel
In flight above the bed.

'I'm not long for this world,'
Said he on our last evening,
'I'll not last the winter,'
And grinned, straining to hear
Whatever reply I made;
And died the following year.

In time the astringent rain
Of those parts will clean
The words from his gravestone
In the crowded cemetery
That overlooks the sea
And his name be mud once again

And his boilers lie like tombs
In the mud of the sea bed
Till the next ice age comes
And the earth he inherited
Is gone like Neanderthal Man
And no records remain.

But the secret bred in the bone
On the dawn strand survives
In other times and lives,
Persisting for the unborn
Like a claw-print in concrete
After the bird has flown.

A Disused Shed in Co. Wexford

Let them not forget us, the weak souls among the asphodels.
          – Seferis, *Mythistorema*, tr. Keeley and Sherrard

(*for J. G. Farrell*)

Even now there are places where a thought might grow —
Peruvian mines, worked out and abandoned
To a slow clock of condensation,
An echo trapped for ever, and a flutter
Of wild-flowers in the lift-shaft,
Indian compounds where the wind dances
And a door bangs with diminished confidence,
Lime crevices behind rippling rain-barrels,
Dog corners for bone burials;
And in a disused shed in Co. Wexford,

Deep in the grounds of a burnt-out hotel,
Among the bathtubs and the washbasins
A thousand mushrooms crowd to a keyhole.
This is the one star in their firmament
Or frames a star within a star.
What should they do there but desire?
So many days beyond the rhododendrons
With the world waltzing in its bowl of cloud,
They have learnt patience and silence
Listening to the rooks querulous in the high wood.

They have been waiting for us in a foetor
Of vegetable sweat since civil war days,
Since the gravel-crunching, interminable departure
Of the expropriated mycologist.
He never came back, and light since then
Is a keyhole rusting gently after rain.
Spiders have spun, flies dusted to mildew
And once a day, perhaps, they have heard something —

A trickle of masonry, a shout from the blue
Or a lorry changing gear at the end of the lane.

There have been deaths, the pale flesh flaking
Into the earth that nourished it;
And nightmares, born of these and the grim
Dominion of stale air and rank moisture.
Those nearest the door grow strong —
'Elbow room! Elbow room!'
The rest, dim in a twilight of crumbling
Utensils and broken pitchers, groaning
For their deliverance, have been so long
Expectant that there is left only the posture.

A half century, without visitors, in the dark —
Poor preparation for the cracking lock
And creak of hinges. Magi, moonmen,
Powdery prisoners of the old regime,
Web-throated, stalked like triffids, racked by drought
And insomnia, only the ghost of a scream
At the flash-bulb firing-squad we wake them with
Shows there is life yet in their feverish forms.
Grown beyond nature now, soft food for worms,
They lift frail heads in gravity and good faith.

They are begging us, you see, in their wordless way,
To do something, to speak on their behalf
Or at least not to close the door again.
Lost people of Treblinka and Pompeii!
'Save us, save us,' they seem to say,
'Let the god not abandon us
Who have come so far in darkness and in pain.
We too had our lives to live.
You with your light meter and relaxed itinerary,
Let not our naive labours have been in vain!'

The Mute Phenomena

(after Nerval)

Your great mistake is to disregard the satire
Bandied among the mute phenomena.
Be strong if you must, your brusque hegemony
Means fuck-all to the somnolent sun-flower
Or the extinct volcano. What do you know
Of the revolutionary theories advanced
By turnips, or the sex-life of cutlery?
Everything is susceptible, Pythagoras said so.

An ordinary common-or-garden brick wall, the kind
For talking to or banging your head on,
Resents your politics and bad draughtsmanship.
God is alive and lives under a stone.
Already in a lost hub-cap is conceived
The ideal society which will replace our own.

Light Music

The glow-worm shows the matin to be near . . .

1. *Architecture*
Twinkletoes in the ballroom,
light music in space.

2. *History*
The blinking puddles
reflected day-long
twilights of misery.

Smoke rose in silence
to the low sky.

3. *Negatives*
Gulls in a rain-dark corn-field,
crows on a sunlit sea.

4. *North Sea*
The terminal light of beaches,
pebbles speckled with oil;
old tins at the tide-line
where a gull blinks on a pole.

5. *Aesthetics*
Neither the tearful taper
nor the withered wick,
that sickly crowd.

But the single bright
landing light
ghosting an iodine cloud.

6. *Please*
I built my house
in a forest far
from the venal roar.

Somebody please
beat a path
to my door.

7. *Rory*
He leads me into
a grainy twilight
of old photographs.

The sun is behind us,
his shadow in mine.

8. *Spring*
Dawn light pearling the branches,
petals freckling the mould,
and the stereo birds.

It is time for the nymphs,
a glimpse of skin in the woods.

9. *Twilight*
A stone at the roadside
watches snow fall
on the silent gate-lodge.

Later the gate shuts
with a clanging of bars;
the stone is one with the stars.

10. *Midnight*
Torchlight swept
the firmament,
chords softly crashed.

But the hedgerows
quiver aghast
when our headlights pass.

11. *Timber*
The whining saw spins free
and the puff of dust
lost in the mist
is the hurt spirit escaping
from the throat of the stricken tree.

12. *Byzantium*
Moth thought of masonry,
daylight mured
from the wine bins.

Silent in one corner
the gleam of a dead star.

13. *Joyce in Paris*
This town a lantern
hung for lovers
in a dark wood
says the blind man.

14. *Mozart*
The Clarinet Concerto
in A, K.622,
the second movement.

Turn it up
so they can hear
on the other planets.

15. *Morphology*
Beans and foetuses,
brains and cauliflowers;
in a shaft of sunlight
a dust of stars.

16. *Enter*
The steel regrets the lock,
a word will open the rock,
the wood awaits your knock.

17. *Dawn Moon*
A slip of soap in the sky,
I do my faint shining
in the golden dawn
of an alien dispensation.

18. *Elpenor*
Edacity in the palace
and in the sandy timber
of my crumbling monument,
its lengthening shadow
pointing towards home.

19. *East Strand*
Tedium of sand and sea
then at the white rocks
a little girl fleetingly,
blazer and ankle-socks.

Sand drifts from a rock
like driven snow, and one
gull attentive to my walk
obscures the winter sun.

20. *Plane*
A vapour trail miles high;
a gleaming spot screams silently
down the morning sky.

21. *Absence*
I wake at night
in a house white
with moonlight.

Somewhere my son,
his vigour, his laughter;
somewhere my daughter.

22. *Night*
A pub sign creaks in the night wind
of a silent seaside resort;
ships, my first loves,
where are you now,
not one of you in port?

23. *Dark Edge*
Gazing west in a London
sunset I imagine
islands of the blest;
their stones still stand,
their washing machines
are manufactured here.

24. *Haven*
First lights in the mist,
one from a yacht cabin:
somebody reading
or playing patience
after his one-man voyage
to the ends of the earth.

25. *Fly-Life*
A fly drones at the window,
inside and gazing out
at a blaze of watery light,
at fields and ocean;
and I imagine
the fly-life of America.

26. *Bluebells*
A forest of bluebells
under the trees
like daffodils in spring:
more forest than the trees themselves.

27. *Loft*
A pigeon trapped, wings beating,
in the shed below
while I sit trapped,
heart beating,
in the loft above.

28. *Waterfront*
I cover the waterfront,
its fish and chips,
while better men
go down to the sea in ships.

29. *Outside*
The sculpted bird-bath and the pine,
the post-box and the telephone line.

30. *Donegal*
The vast clouds migrate
above turf-stacks
and a dangling gate.

A tiny bike squeaks
into the wind.

31. *Smoke*
Vertical, horizontal,
the smoke of last resorts.

32. *Rogue Leaf*
Believe it or not
I hung on all winter
outfacing wind and snow.

Now that spring
comes and the birds sing
I am letting go.

33. *Revelation*
A colour the fish know
we do not know so
long have we been ashore.

When that colour
shines in the rainbow
there will be no more sea.

34. *Flying*
A wand of sunlight
touches the rush-hour
like the finger of heaven.

A land of cumulus
seen from above
is the life to come.

Midsummer

Today the longest day and the people have gone.
The sun concentrates on the kitchen garden
with the bright intensity of June.
The birds we heard singing at dawn
are dozing among the leaves
while a faint soap waits its turn
in a blue sky, strange to the afternoon —
one eye on the pasture where cows roam
and one on the thin line between land
and sea, where the quietest waves
will break there when the people have gone home.

Ford Manor

Even on the quietest days the distant
growl of cars remains persistent,
reaching us in this airy box
we share with the field-mouse and the fox;
but she drifts in maternity blouses
among crack-paned greenhouses —
a smiling Muse come back to life,
part child, part mother, and part wife.

Even on the calmest nights the fitful
prowl of planes is seldom still
where Gatwick tilts to guide them home
from Tokyo, New York or Rome;
yet even today the earth disposes
bluebells, roses and primroses,
the dawn throat-whistle of a thrush
deep in the dripping lilac bush.

Penshurst Place

The bright drop quivering on a thorn
in the rich silence after rain,
lute music in the orchard aisles,
the paths ablaze with daffodils,
intrigue and venery in the air
à l'ombre des jeunes filles en fleurs,
the iron hand and the velvet glove —
come live with me and be my love.

A pearl face, numinously bright,
shining in silence of the night,
a muffled crash of smouldering logs,
bad dreams of courtiers and of dogs,
the Spanish ships around Kinsale,
the screech-owl and the nightingale,
the falcon and the turtle dove —
come live with me and be my love.

How to Live

(Horace, *Odes* I, II)
Don't waste your time, Leuconoé, living in fear and hope
of the imprevisable future; forget the horoscope.
Accept whatever happens. Whether the gods allow
us fifty winters more or drop us at this one now
which flings the high Tyrrhenian waves on the stone piers,
decant your wine. The days are more fun than the years
which pass us by while we discuss them. Act with zest
one day at a time, and never mind the rest.

Ovid in Love

1. (*Amores* I, V)
The day being humid and my head
heavy, I stretched out on a bed.
The open window to the right
reflected woodland-watery light,
a keyed-up silence as of dawn
or dusk, the vibrant and uncertain
hour when a brave girl might undress
and caper naked on the grass.
You entered in a muslin gown,
bare-footed, your fine braids undone,
a fabled goddess with an air
as if in heat yet debonair.
Aroused, I grabbed and roughly tore
until your gown squirmed on the floor.
Oh, you resisted, but like one
who knows resistance is in vain;
and, when you stood revealed, my eyes
feasted on shoulders, breasts and thighs.
I held you hard and down you slid
beside me, as we knew you would.
Oh, come to me again as then you did!

2. (*Amores*, II, XI)
This strange sea-going craze began
with Jason. Pine from Pelion,
weathered and shaped, was first to brave
the whirlpool and the whistling wave.
I wish the *Argo* had gone down
and seafaring remained unknown;
for now Corinna, scornful of
her safety and my vigilant love,
intends to tempt the winds and go
cruising upon the treacherous blue

waters where no shade-giving ilex,
temple or marble pavement breaks
with its enlightened artistry
the harsh monotony of the sea.
Walk on the beach where you may hear
the whorled conch whisper in your ear;
dance in the foam, but never trust
the water higher than your waist.
I'm serious. Listen to those with real
experience of life under sail;
believe their frightening anecdotes
of rocks and gales and splintered boats.
You won't be able to change your mind
when once your ship is far from land
and the most sanguine seamen cease
their banter as the waves increase.
How pale you'd grow if Triton made
the waters crash around your head —
so much more comfortable ashore
reading, or practising the lyre!
Still, if you're quite determined, God
preserve you from a watery bed:
Nereus' nymphs would be disgraced
if my Corinna should be lost.
Think of me when your shrinking craft
is a poignant pinpoint in the aft-
ernoon, and again when homeward bound
with canvas straining in the wind.
I'll be the first one at the dock
to meet the ship that brings you back.
I'll carry you ashore and burn
thank-offerings for your safe return.
Right there we'll make a bed of sand,
a table of a sand-dune, and
over the wine you'll give a vivid

sketch of the perils you survived —
how, faced with a tempestuous sea,
you hung on tight and thought of me!
Make it up if you like, as I
invent this pleasant fantasy . . .

from *The Drunken Boat*

(after Rimbaud)

Hearing the thunder of the intransitive weirs
I felt my guiding tow-ropes slacken; crazed
Apaches, yelping, nailed my gondoliers
Naked to stakes where fiery feathers blazed.

Not that I cared. Relieved of the dull weight
Of cautious crew and inventoried cargo —
Phlegmatic flax, quotidian grain — I let
The current carry me where I chose to go.

Deaf to the furious whisperings of the sand,
My heart rose to a tidal detonation;
Pensinulas, ripped screaming from the land,
Crashed in a stinging mist of exultation.

Storms smiled on my salt sea-morning sleep.
I danced, light as a cork, nine nights or more,
Upon the intractable, man-trundling deep,
Contemptuous of the blinking lights ashore.

Juice of the oceans, tart as unripe fruit,
Burst on my spruce boards in tongues of brine
That tore the spinning binnacle from its root,
Rinsing the curdled puke and the blue wine.

And then I was submerged in a sea-poem
Infused with milky stars, gulped the profound
Viridian where, disconsolate and calm,
Rapt faces drifted past of the long drowned.

I saw skies split by lightning, granite waves
Shaking the earth, ambrosial dusks and dawns,
Day risen aloft, a multitude of doves —
And, with the naked eye, vouchsafed visions;

Watched horizontal orbs, like spotlights trained
On some barbaric tragedy of old,
Direct their peacock rays along the sun-blind
Waters, and heard their clattering slats unfold.

I dreamed the emerald snow of dazzling chasms,
Kisses ascending to the eyes of the sea,
The circulation of mysterious plasms
And mornings loud with phosphorous harmony.

Trembling, I heard volcanic eructations,
A thrash of behemoths . . . But now, my ears
Weary of this crescendo of sensations,
I thought of Europe and its ancient towers.

Delirious capes! Strewn archipelagoes!
Do you nurse there in your galactic foam
The glistening bodies of obscure flamingoes
Tranced in a prescience of the life to come?

Meuse of the cloud-canals, I would ask of you
Only the pond where, on a quiet evening,
An only child launches a toy canoe
As frail and pitiful as a moth in spring.

Three Poems by Philippe Jaccottet

1. *The Voice*
What is it that sings when the other voices are silent?
Whose is that pure, deaf voice, that sibilant song?
Is it down the road on a snow-covered lawn
or close at hand, aware of an audience?
This is the mysterious first bird of dawn.
Do you hear the voice increase in volume
and, as a March wind quickens a creaking tree,
sing mildly to us without fear,
content in the fact of death? Do you hear?
What does it sing in the grey dawn? Nobody knows
but the voice is audible only to those
whose hearts seek neither possession nor victory.

2. *Ignorance*
The older I grow the more ignorant I become,
the longer I live the less I possess or control.
All I have is a little space, snow-dark
or glittering, never inhabited.
Where is the giver, the guide, the guardian?
I sit in my room and am silent. Silence
arrives like a servant to tidy things up
while I wait for the lies to disperse.
And what remains to this dying man
that so well prevents him from dying?
What does he find to say to the four walls?
I hear him talking still, and his words
come in with the dawn, imperfectly understood —

'Love, like fire, can only reveal its brightness
on the failure and the beauty of burnt wood.'

3. *Words in the Air*
The clear air said, 'I was your home once
but other guests have taken your place;
where will you go who liked it here so much?
You looked at me through the thick dust
of the earth, and your eyes were known to me.
You sang sometimes, you even whispered low
to someone else who was often asleep,
you told her the light of the earth
was too pure not to point a direction
which somehow avoided death. You imagined
yourself advancing in that direction;
but now I no longer hear you. What have you done?
Above all, what is your lover going to think?'

And she, his friend, replied through tears of happiness,
'He has changed into the shade that pleased him best.'

Soles

'I caught four soles this morning,'
said the man with the beard;
cloud shifted and a sun-
shaft pierced the sea.
Fisher of soles, did you reflect
the water you walked on
contains so very many souls,
the living and the dead,
you could never begin to count them?

Somewhere a god waits,
rod in hand,
to add you to their number.

Autobiographies

(*for Maurice Leitch*)

1. *The Home Front*
While the frozen armies trembled
At the gates of Leningrad
They took me home in a taxi
And laid me in my cot,
And there I slept again
With siren and black-out;

And slept under the stairs
Beside the light meter
When bombs fell on the city;
So I never saw the sky
Ablaze with a fiery glow,
Searchlights roaming the stars.

But I do remember one time
(I must have been four then)
Being held up to the window
For a victory parade —
Soldiers, sailors and airmen
Lining the Antrim Road;

And, later, hide-and-seek
Among the air-raid shelters,
The last ration coupons,
Oranges and bananas,
Forage caps and badges
And packets of Lucky Strike.

Gracie Fields on the radio!
Americans in the art-deco
Milk bars! The released Jews
Blinking in shocked sunlight . . .

A male child in a garden
Clutching the *Empire News*.

2. *The Lost Girls*
'In ancient shadows and twilights
Where childhood had strayed'
I ran round in the playground
Of Skegoneill Primary School
During the lunch break,
Pretending to be a plane.

For months I would dawdle home
At a respectful distance
Behind the teacher's daughter,
Eileen Boyd, who lived
In a house whose back garden
Was visible from my window.

I watched her on summer evenings,
A white dress picking flowers,
Her light, graceful figure
Luminous and remote.
We never exchanged greetings;
Her house was bigger than ours.

She married an older man
And went to live in Kenya.
Perhaps she is there still
Complaining about 'the natives'.
It would be nice to know;
But who can re-live their lives?

Eileen Boyd, Hazel and Heather
Thompson, Patricia King —

The lost girls in a ring
On a shadowy school playground
Like the nymphs dancing together
In the *Allegory of Spring*.

3. *The Last Resort*
Salad-and-sand sandwiches
And dead gulls on the beach;
Ice-cream in the Arcadia,
Rain lashing the windows;
Dull days in the harbour,
Sunday mornings in church.

One hot July fortnight
In the Strandmore Hotel
I watched the maid climb
The stairs, and went to my room
Quivering with excitement,
Aroused for the first time.

Years later, the same dim
Resort has grown dimmer
As if some centrifugal
Force, summer by summer,
Has moved it ever farther
From an imagined centre.

The guest-houses are crazy
For custom; but the risen
People are playing football
On the sands of Tenerife,
Far from the unrelaxing
Scenes of sectarian strife.

Yet the place really existed
And still can crack a smile
Should a sunbeam pick out
Your grimy plastic cup
And consecrate your vile
Bun with its parting light.

4. *The Bicycle*
There was a bicycle, a fine
Raleigh with five gears
And racing handlebars.
It stood at the front door
Begging to be mounted;
The frame shone in the sun.

I became like a character
In *The Third Policeman*, half
Human, half bike, my life
A series of dips and ridges,
Happiness a free-wheeling
Past fragrant hawthorn hedges.

Cape and sou'wester streamed
With rain when I rode to school
Side-tracking the bus routes.
Night after night I dreamed
Of valves, pumps, sprockets,
Reflectors and repair kits.

Soon there were long rides
In the country, wet week-ends
Playing snap in the kitchens
Of mountain youth-hostels,

Day-runs to Monaghan,
Rough and exotic roads.

It went with me to Dublin
Where I sold it the same winter;
But its wheels still sing
In the memory, stars that turn
About an eternal centre,
The bright spokes glittering.

A Kensington Notebook

I
South Lodge is blue-
Plaqued where Ford set out
His toy soldiers on the
Razed table of art.

There was a great good place
Of clean-limbed young men
And high-minded virgins,
Cowslip and celandine;

Henry James to be visited,
Lawrence to be prized,
Conrad to be instructed,
Yeats to be lionized.

Sussex chirped in the sun.
A man could stand up
Then, and a woman too,
Before the thunder-clap.

(Intrigue at German spas,
Bombast on golf-courses,
Perfidy in the ministries,
Bitches in country houses . . .)

What price the dewy-eyed
Pelagianism of home
To a lost generation
Dumbfounded on the Somme?

An old cod in a land
Unfit for heroes,
He consecrates his new life to
Mnemosyne and Eros.

'The last of England'
Crumbles in the rain
As he embarks for
Paris and Michigan.

II
The operantics of
Provence and Languedoc
Shook the Gaudier marbles
At No. 10 Church Walk

Where 'Ezra Pound, M.A.,
Author of *Personae*',
Twitched his nostrils and
Invisible antennae;

Rihaku, nursed Osiris'
Torn limbs; came to know
Holland St. stone by stone
As he knew San Zeno —

That 'ultimate perfection'
At Sirmione, a place
Of light 'almost solid', each
Column signed at the base.

Meanwhile his Sunday mornings
Are scrambled by the din
Of bells from St. Mary
Abbots down the lane.

(Not Dowland, not Purcell
'The age demanded',
But the banalities
Of the *Evening Standard*.)

The Spirit of Romance
Flowered briefly there
Among jade animals;
And years later where,

Confucius of the dooryard,
Prophet of *τὸ καλόν*,
He drawls 'treason' into
A Roman microphone.

III
Asquith was not amused
When the editor of *Blast*,
Dining with the Prince of Wales
At Lady Drogheda's, placed

A pearl-handled revolver
On the white table-cloth —
Anarchy masquerading
As art, dangerous both.

Aesthetic bombardiering
Prefigured the real thing,
The *monstre gai* in a vortex
Of 'stone laughing' —

A moonscape, trees like gibbets,
Shrapnel, wire, the thud
Of howitzers, spike-helmeted
Skeletons in the mud.

War artist, he depicts
The death-throes of an era
While Orpen glorifies
Haig, Gough etc.;

Holed up in Holland Park,
Practises an implacable
Ordnance of the body
And casts out the soul.

Vitriol versus cocoa,
Adam versus the Broad
Church of received opinion,
He goads the Apes of God.

Nietzschean politics,
Urbane rejection, debt,
Six years of Canadian
Exile, psychic defeat.

IV
No more parades . . .
Ghostly bugles sound
The 'Last Post'; the last fox
Has gone to ground

Beneath the shadow of
A nuclear power plant,
Its whirling radar dishes
Anxious and vehement.

Empire is fugitive
And the creative thrust.
Only the chimps remain;
The rest is dust.

Tragic? No, 'available
Reality' was increased,
The sacred flame kept alive,
The Muse not displeased;

And if one or two
Were short on ἀγάπη,
What was that to the evil
Done in their day?

Ford dies abroad,
A marginal figure still;
And Lewis, self-condemned,
Eyeless in Notting Hill.

Pound, released, reads
To his grandchildren; 'helps'
With the garden; dozes off in a high
Silence of the Alps —

Un rameur, finally,
Sur le fleuve des morts,
Poling his profile toward
What farther shore?

Going Home

*Pure, bracing ventilation they must have up there at all times,
indeed: one may guess the power of the north wind . . . by a
range of gaunt thorns all stretching their limbs one way, as if
craving alms of the sun.*

— Emily Brontë, *Wuthering Heights*

(*for John Hewitt*)

I am saying goodbye to the trees,
The beech, the cedar, the elm,
The mild woods of these parts
Misted with car exhaust
And sawdust, and the last
Gasps of the poisoned nymphs.

I have watched girls walking
And children playing under
Lilac and rhododendron,
And me flicking my ash
Into the rose bushes
As if I owned the place;

As if the trees responded
To my ignorant admiration
Before dawn when the branches
Glitter at first light,
Or later on when the finches
Disappear for the night;

And often thought if I lived
Long enough in this house
I would turn into a tree
Like somebody in Ovid
— A small tree certainly
But a tree nevertheless —

Perhaps befriend the oak,
The chestnut and the yew,
Become a home for birds,
A shelter for the nymphs,
And gaze out over the downs
As if I belonged here too.

But where I am going the trees
Are few and far between.
No richly forested slopes,
Not for a long time,
And few winking woodlands.
There are no nymphs to be seen.

Out there you would look in vain
For a rose bush; but find,
Rooted in stony ground,
A last stubborn growth
Battered by constant rain
And twisted by the sea-wind

With nothing to recommend it
But its harsh tenacity
Between the blinding windows
And the forests of the sea,
As if its very existence
Were a reason to continue.

Crone, crow, scarecrow,
Its worn fingers scrabbling
At a torn sky, it stands
On the edge of everything
Like a burnt-out angel
Raising petitionary hands.

Grotesque by day, at twilight
An almost tragic figure
Of anguish and despair,
It merges into the funeral
Cloud-continent of night
As if it belongs there.

The Chinese Restaurant in Portrush

Before the first visitor comes the spring
Softening the sharp air of the coast
In time for the first 'invasion'.
Today the place is as it might have been,
Gentle and almost hospitable. A girl
Strides past the Northern Counties Hotel,
Light-footed, swinging a book-bag,
And the doors that were shut all winter
Against the north wind and the sea mist
Lie open to the street, where one
By one the gulls go window-shopping
And an old wolfhound dozes in the sun.

While I sit with my paper and prawn chow mein
Under a framed photograph of Hong Kong
The proprietor of the Chinese restaurant
Stands at the door as if the world were young,
Watching the first yacht hoist a sail
— An ideogram on sea-cloud — and the light
Of heaven upon the mountains of Donegal;
And whistles a little tune, dreaming of home.

Rock Music

The ocean glittered quietly in the moonlight
While heavy metal rocked the discotheques;
Space-age Hondas farted half the night,
Fired by the prospect of fortuitous sex.
I sat late at the window, blind with rage,
And listened to the tumult down below,
Trying to concentrate on the printed page
As if such obsolete bumph could save us now.

Next morning, wandering on the strand, I heard
Left-over echoes of the night before
Dwindle to echoes, and a single bird
Drown with a whistle that residual roar.
Rock music started up on every side —
Whisper of algae, click of stone on stone,
A thousand limpets left by the ebb-tide
Unanimous in their silent inquisition.

The Blackbird

One morning in the month of June
I was coming out of this door
And found myself in a garden,
A sanctuary of light and air
Transplanted from the Hesperides,
No sound of machinery anywhere,
When from a bramble bush a hidden
Blackbird suddenly gave tongue,
Its diffident, resilient song
Breaking the silence of the seas.

The Attic

(*for John and Evelyn Montague*)

Under the night window
   A dockyard fluorescence,
Muse-light on the city,
   A world of heightened sense.

At work in your attic
   Up here under the roof —
Listen, can you hear me
   Turning over a new leaf?

Silent by ticking lamplight
   I stare at the blank spaces,
Reflecting the composure
   Of patient surfaces —

I who know nothing
   Scribbling on the off-chance,
Darkening the white page,
   Cultivating my ignorance.

The Old Snaps

I keep your old snaps in my bottom drawer —
The icons of a more than personal love.
Look, three sisters out of Chekhov
('When will we ever go to Moscow?')
Ranged on the steps of the school-house
Where their mother is head teacher,
Out on the rocks, or holding down their hair
In a high wind on a North Antrim shore.

Later, yourself alone among sand-hills
Striking a slightly fictional pose,
Life-ready and impervious to harm
In your wind-blown school uniform,
While the salt sea air fills
Your young body with ozone
And fine sand trickles into your shoes.
I think I must have known you even then.

We went to Moscow, and we will again.
Meanwhile we walk on the strand
And smile as if for the first time
While the children play in the sand.
We have never known a worse winter
But the old snaps are always there,
Framed for ever in your heart and mine
Where no malicious hands can twist or tear.

Dawn at St. Patrick's

There is an old
statue in the courtyard
that weeps, like Niobe, its sorrow in stone.
The griefs of the ages she has made her own.
Her eyes are rain-washed but not hard,
her body is covered in mould,
the garden overgrown.

One by one
the first lights come on,
those that haven't been on all night.
Christmas, the harshly festive, has come and gone.
No snow, but the rain pours down
in the first hour before dawn,
before daylight.

Swift's home
for 'fools and mad' has become
the administrative block. Much there
has remained unchanged for many a long year —
stairs, chairs, Georgian windows shafting light and dust,
radiantly white the marble bust
of the satirist;

but the real
hospital is a cheerful
modern extension at the back
hung with restful reproductions of Dufy, Klee and Braque.
Television, Russian fiction, snooker with the staff,
a snifter of Lucozade, a paragraph
of *Newsweek* or the *Daily Mail*

are my daily routine
during the festive season.
They don't lock the razors here
as in Bowditch Hall. We have remained upright —
though, to be frank, the Christmas dinner scene,
with grown men in their festive gear,
was a sobering sight.

I watch the last
planes of the year go past,
silently climbing a cloud-lit sky.
Earth-bound, soon I'll be taking a train to Cork
and trying to get back to work
at my sea-lit, fort-view desk
in the turf-smoky dusk.

Meanwhile,
next-door, a visiting priest
intones to a faithful dormitory.
I sit on my Protestant bed, a make-believe existentialist,
and stare at the clouds of unknowing. We style,
as best we may, our private destiny;
or so it seems to me

as I chew my thumb
and try to figure out
what brought me to my present state —
an 'educated man', a man of consequence, no bum
but one who has hardly grasped what life is about,
if anything. My children, far away,
don't know where I am today,

in a Dublin asylum
with a paper whistle and a mince pie,
my bits and pieces making a home from home.
I pray to the rain-clouds that they never come
where their lost father lies; that their mother thrives;
   and that I
may measure up to them
before I die.

Soon a new year
will be here demanding, as before,
modest proposals, resolute resolutions, a new leaf,
new leaves. This is the story of my life,
the story of all lives everywhere,
mad fools wherever they are,
in here or out there.

Light and sane
I shall walk down to the train,
into that world whose sanity we know,
like Swift, to be a fiction and a show.
The clouds part, the rain ceases, the sun
casts now upon everyone
its ancient shadow.

Beyond the Pale

(after Corbière)

A ruined convent on the Breton coast —
Gathering place for wind and mist,
Where the donkeys of Finistère
Sheltered against the ivied walls,
Masonry pitted with such gaping holes
There was no knowing which one was the door.

Solitary but upright, in undiminished pride,
The *cailleach* of the countryside,
Roof like a hat askew, she stood
Remembering her past — a den
For smugglers and night-walkers now,
For stray dogs, rats, lovers and excisemen.

A feral poet lived in the one-eyed tower,
His wings clipped, having settled there
Among vigilant and lugubrious owls.
He respected their rights however,
He, the only owl who paid —
A thousand francs a year and a new door.

The locals he ignored, though not they him.
Sharp eyes saw from the road below
Where he dithered at a window.
The priest believed he was a leper
But the mayor said, 'What can I do?
He's probably a foreigner of some kind.'

The women, though, were not slow to discover
That this barely visible recluse
Shared the place with a lover

Whom he referred to as his 'Muse' —
Parisians, no doubt, the pair of them!
But she lay low, and the storm blew over.

He was, in fact, one of life's fugitives,
An amateur hermit blown in with the leaves
Who had lived too long by a southern sea.
Pursued by doctors and tax inspectors
He had come here in search of peace,
To die alone or live in contumacy —

An artist or philosopher, after a fashion,
Who chose to live beyond the pale.
He had his hammock, his barrel-organ,
His little dog Fidèle
And, no less faithful, gentle and grave as he,
A lifelong intimate he called Ennui.

He dreamed his life, his dream the tide that flows
Rattling among the stones, the tide that ebbs.
Sometimes he stood there as if listening —
For what? For the wind to rise,
For the sea to sing?
Or for some half-forgotten voice? Who knows?

Does he know himself? Up there on the exposed
Roof of himself, does he forget how soon
And how completely death unmakes
The dead? He, restless ghost,
Is it perhaps his own lost
Contumacious spirit that he seeks?

Not far, not far, she after whom you bell,
Stag of St. Hubert! All may yet be well!

. . . A door banged in his head
And he heard the slow tread of hexameters . . .

Not knowing how to live, he learned how to survive
And, not knowing how to die, he wrote:
                                        'My love,
I write, therefore I am. When I said goodbye
To you, it was life I was saying goodbye to —
You who wept for us so that I wanted
To stay and weep beside you. However
It's too late now, the die is cast.
Oh yes, I'm still here, but as if erased.
I am dying slowly into legend;
Spiders spin in the brain where a star burned.

'Come and help me die; from your room
You'll be able to see my harvest fields
(A few firs shivering in the wind)
And the wild heather in full bloom
(Well, bundled around the fireplace).
You can gulp your fill of the sea air
(It's nearly taking the roof off)
And climb to sleep by a golden stair
(Lit by a single candle)
While the sea murmurs of shipwrecks —
Tenebrae for the wild ducks.

'And the nights! Nights for orgies in the tower!
Romeo nights that no sun rises on!
Nights of the nightingale in the gale!
Can you hear my Aeolian door squeal
And the rats whirl in the attic?

'You inhabit my dreams and my day-dreams; over
Everything, like a spirit, you hover.

You are my solitude, my owls
And my weathercock; the wind howls
Your name when my shutter
Shakes, and the shadow thrown
For an instant on the bare wall is yours;
Yet when I turn my head it disappears.
A knock at the door! Is that
Your knock there, calling me? No, only a rat.

'I've taken my lyre and my barrel-organ
To serenade you — ridiculous!
Come and cry if I've made you laugh,
Come and laugh if I've made you cry,
Come and play at misery
Taken from life: "Love in a Cottage"!
It rains in my hearth, it rains fire in my heart;
And now my fire is dead, and I have no more light . . . '

His lamp went out; he opened the shutter.
The sun rose; he gazed at his letter,
Laughed and then tore it up . . .

      The little bits of white
Looked, in the mist, like gulls in flight.

Everything Is Going To Be All Right

How should I not be glad to contemplate
the clouds clearing beyond the dormer window
and a high tide reflected on the ceiling?
There will be dying, there will be dying,
but there is no need to go into that.
The poems flow from the hand unbidden
and the hidden source is the watchful heart.
The sun rises in spite of everything
and the far cities are beautiful and bright.
I lie here in a riot of sunlight
watching the day break and the clouds flying.
Everything is going to be all right.

Heraclitus on Rivers

Nobody steps into the same river twice.
The same river is never the same
Because that is the nature of water.
Similarly your changing metabolism
Means that you are no longer you.
The cells die, and the precise
Configuration of the heavenly bodies
When she told you she loved you
Will not come again in this lifetime.

You will tell me that you have executed
A monument more lasting than bronze;
But even bronze is perishable.
Your best poem, you know the one I mean,
The very language in which the poem
Was written, and the idea of language,
All these things will pass away in time.

The Sea in Winter

Nous ne sommes pas au monde;
la vraie vie est absente.
                    — Rimbaud

(for Desmond O'Grady)

Desmond, what of the blue nights,
the ultramarines and violets
of your white island in the south,
'far-shining star of dark-blue earth',
and the boat-lights in the tiny port
where we drank so much retsina?
Up here where the air is thinner
in a draughty bungalow in Portstewart

beside my 'distant northern sea',
I imagine a moon of Asia Minor
bright on your nightly industry.
Sometimes, rounding the cliff top
at dusk, under the convent wall,
and finding the little town lit up
as if for some island festival,
I pretend not to be here at all;

that the shop-fronts along the prom,
whose fluorescence blinds the foam
and shingle, are the dancing lights
of Náousa — those calescent nights! —
that these frosty pavements are
the stones of that far-shining star;
that the cold, glistening sea-mist
eclipses Naxos to the east.

But morning scatters down the strand
relics of last night's gale-force wind;
far out, the Atlantic faintly breaks,
sea-weed exhales among the rocks,
and fretfully the spent winds fan
the cenotaph and the lifeboat mine;
from door to door the Ormo van
delivers, while the stars decline.

Portstewart, Portrush, Portballintrae —
un beau pays mal habité,
policed by rednecks in dark cloth
and roving gangs of tartan youth.
No place for a gentleman like you.
The good, the beautiful and the true
have a tough time of it; and yet
there *is* that Hebridean sunset,

and a strange poetry of decay
charms the condemned hotels by day,
while in the dark hours the rattle
of a cat knocking over a milk-bottle
on a distant doorstep by moonlight
can set you thinking half the night.
The stars of Nineveh and Tyre
shine still on the Harbour Bar.

You too have known the curious sense
of working on the circumference —
the midnight oil, familiar sea,
elusive dawn epiphany,
faith that the trivia doodled here
will bear their fruit sometime, somewhere;
that the long winter months may bring
gifts to the goddess in the spring.

The sea in winter, where she walks,
vents its displeasure on the rocks;
the something rotten in the state
infects the innocent; the spite
mankind has brought to this infernal
backwater destroys the soul;
it sneaks into the daily life,
sunders the husband from the wife.

Is that the prodigal son in *Ghosts*,
back on the grim, arthritic coasts
of the cold north, where he finds himself
unnerved, his talents on the shelf,
slumped in a deck-chair, full of pills,
while light dies in the choral hills —
on antebuse and mogadon
recovering, crying out for the sun?

Or Theseus in the open air
who knew the sphincter-opening fear
of chthonic echoes, and now brings
his gaze to rest on simple things
of marble, quartz and cedar-wood,
a spaniel sprawling in the shade,
while a dim frieze of laughing girls
and dolphins ripples on the tiles?

Why am I always staring out
of windows, preferably from a height?
I think the redemptive enterprise
of water — hold it to the light! —
yet distance is the vital bond
between the window and the wind,
while equilibrium demands
a cold eye and deliberate hands.

Sometimes, a deliberate exercise,
I study the tide-warp in the glass,
the wandering rain-drops, casual flies;
but still, beyond the shivering grass,
the creamy seas and turbulent skies
race in the bloodstream where they pass
like metaphors for human life —
sex, death and Heraclitean strife.

A fine view may console the heart
with analogues for one kind of art —
chaste winter-gardens of the sea
glimmering to infinity;
yet in those greasy depths will stir
no tengo mas que dar te where
Jehovah blew and, ship by ship,
consigned their ordnance to the deep.

And all the time I have my doubts
about this verse-making. The shouts
of souls in torment round the town
at closing time make as much sense
and carry as much significance
as these lines carefully set down.
All farts in a biscuit tin, in truth —
faint cries, sententious or uncouth.

Yet they are most of life, and not
the laid-back metropolitan lot,
the 'great' photographer and the hearty
critic at the cocktail party.
Most live like these with wire and dust
and dream machinery. My disgust
at their pathetic animation
merely reflects my own condition;

for I am trapped as much as they
in my own idiom. One day,
perhaps, the words will find their mark
and leave a brief glow on the dark,
effect mutations of dead things
into a form that nearly sings —
waste paper left to indicate
our long day's journey into night.

But let me never forget the weird
haecceity of this strange sea-board,
the heroism and cowardice
of living on the edge of space,
or ever again contemptuously
refuse its plight; for history
ignores those who ignore it, not
the ignorant whom it begot.

To start from scratch, to make it new,
forsake the grey skies for the blue,
to find the narrow road to the deep
north the road to Damascus, leap
before we look! The ideal future
shines out of our better nature,
dimly visible from afar:
'The sun is but a morning star.'

One day, the day each one conceives —
the day the Dying Gaul revives,
the day the girl among the trees
strides through our wrecked technologies,
the stones speak out, the rainbow ends,
the wine goes round among the friends,
the lost are found, the parted lovers
lie at peace beneath the covers.

Meanwhile the given life goes on;
there is nothing new under the sun.
The dogs bark and the caravan
glides mildly by; and if the dawn
that wakes us now should also find us
cured of our ancient colour-blindness . . .
I who know nothing go to teach
while a new day crawls up the beach.

'Songs of Praise'

Tonight, their simple church grown glamorous,
The proud parishioners of the outlying parts
Lift up their hymn-books and their hearts
To please the outside-broadcast cameras.
The darkness deepens; day draws to a close;
A well-bred sixth-former yawns with her nose.

Outside, the hymn dies among rocks and dunes.
Conflicting rhythms of the incurious sea,
Not even contemptuous of these tiny tunes,
Take over where our thin ascriptions fail.
Down there the silence of the laboratory,
Trombone dispatches of the beleaguered whale.

Courtyards in Delft

— Pieter de Hooch, 1659

(*for Gordon Woods*)

Oblique light on the trite, on brick and tile —
Immaculate masonry, and everywhere that
Water tap, that broom and wooden pail
To keep it so. House-proud, the wives
Of artisans pursue their thrifty lives
Among scrubbed yards, modest but adequate.
Foliage is sparse, and clings. No breeze
Ruffles the trim composure of those trees.

No spinet-playing emblematic of
The harmonies and disharmonies of love;
No lewd fish, no fruit, no wide-eyed bird
About to fly its cage while a virgin
Listens to her seducer, mars the chaste
Perfection of the thing and the thing made.
Nothing is random, nothing goes to waste.
We miss the dirty dog, the fiery gin.

That girl with her back to us who waits
For her man to come home for his tea
Will wait till the paint disintegrates
And ruined dikes admit the esurient sea;
Yet this is life too, and the cracked
Out-house door a verifiable fact
As vividly mnemonic as the sunlit
Railings that front the houses opposite.

I lived there as a boy and know the coal
Glittering in its shed, late-afternoon
Lambency informing the deal table,
The ceiling cradled in a radiant spoon.

I must be lying low in a room there,
A strange child with a taste for verse,
While my hard-nosed companions dream of fire
And sword upon parched veldt and fields of rain-swept gorse.

Rathlin

A long time since the last scream cut short —
Then an unnatural silence; and then
A natural silence, slowly broken
By the shearwater, by the sporadic
Conversation of crickets, the bleak
Reminder of a metaphysical wind.
Ages of this, till the report
Of an outboard motor at the pier
Shatters the dream-time, and we land
As if we were the first visitors here.

The whole island a sanctuary where amazed
Oneiric species whistle and chatter,
Evacuating rock-face and cliff-top.
Cerulean distance, an oceanic haze —
Nothing but sea-smoke to the ice-cap
And the odd somnolent freighter.
Bombs doze in the housing estates
But here they are through with history —
Custodians of a lone light which repeats
One simple statement to the turbulent sea.

A long time since the unspeakable violence —
Since Somhairle Buidh, powerless on the mainland,
Heard the screams of the Rathlin women
Borne to him, seconds later, upon the wind.
Only the cry of the shearwater
And the roar of the outboard motor
Disturb the singular peace. Spray-blind,
We leave here the infancy of the race,
Unsure among the pitching surfaces
Whether the future lies before us or behind.

Derry Morning

The mist clears and the cavities
Glow black in the rubbled city's
Broken mouth. An early crone,
Muse of a fitful revolution
Wasted by the fray, she sees
Her *aisling* falter in the breeze,
Her oak-grove vision hesitate
By empty wharf and city gate.

Here it began, and here at last
It fades into the finite past
Or seems to: clattering shadows whop
Mechanically over pub and shop.
A strangely pastoral silence rules
The shining roofs and murmuring schools;
For this is how the centuries work —
Two steps forward, one step back.

Hard to believe this tranquil place,
Its desolation almost peace,
Was recently a boom-town wild
With expectation, each unscheduled
Incident a measurable
Tremor on the Richter Scale
Of world events, each vibrant scene
Translated to the drizzling screen.

What of the change envisioned here,
The quantum leap from fire to fear?
Smoke from a thousand chimneys strains
One way beneath the returning rains
That shroud the bomb-sites, while the fog
Of time receives the ideologue.
A Russian freighter bound for home
Mourns to the city in its gloom.

North Wind: Portrush

I shall never forget the wind
On this benighted coast.
It works itself into the mind
Like the high keen of a lost
Lear-spirit in agony
Condemned for eternity

To wander cliff and cove
Without comfort, without love.
It whistles off the stars
And the existential, black
Face of the cosmic dark.
We crouch to roaring fires.

Yet there are mornings when,
Even in midwinter, sunlight
Flares, and a rare stillness
Lies upon roof and garden —
Each object eldritch-bright,
The sea scarred but at peace.

Then, from the ship we say
Is the lit town where we live
(Our whiskey-and-forecast world),
A smaller ship that sheltered
All night in the restless bay
Will weigh anchor and leave.

What did they think of us
During their brief sojourn?
A string of lights on the prom
Dancing mad in the storm —
Who lives in such a place?
And will they ever return?

But the shops open at nine
As they have always done,
The wrapped-up bourgeoisie
Hardened by wind and sea.
The newspapers are late
But the milk shines in its crate.

Everything swept so clean
By tempest, wind and rain!
Elated, you might believe
That this was the first day —
A false sense of reprieve,
For the climate is here to stay.

So best prepare for the worst
That chaos and old night
Can do to us. Were we not
Raised on such expectations,
Our hearts starred with frost
Through countless generations?

Elsewhere the olive grove,
Le déjeuner sur l'herbe,
Poppies and parasols,
Blue skies and mythic love.
Here only the stricken souls
No spring can unperturb.

Prospero and his people never
Came to these stormy parts;
Few do who have the choice.
Yet, blasting the subtler arts,
That weird, plaintive voice
Choirs now and for ever.

An Old Lady

The old motorbike she was
The first woman in those
Parts to ride — a noble
Norton — disintegrates
With rusty iron gates
In some abandoned stable;

But lives in sepia shades
Where an emancipated
Country schoolteacher
Of nineteen thirty-eight
Grins from her frame before
Broaching the mountain roads.

Forty years later she
Shakes slack on the fire
To douse it while she goes
Into Bushmills to buy
Groceries and newspaper
And exchange courtesies.

Then back to a pot of tea
And the early-evening news
(Some fresh atrocity);
Washes up to the sound
Of a chat-show, one phrase
Of Bach going round and round

In her head as she stares
Out at the wintry moon
And thinks of her daughters
So very far away —
Although the telephone
Makes nonsense of that today.

Out there beyond the edge
Of the golf-course tosses
The ghost of the *Girona*,
Flagship of the Armada —
History. Does the knowledge
Alter the world she sees?

Or do her thoughts travel
By preference among
Memories of her naval
Husband, thirty years
Drowned, the watercolours
And instruments unstrung?

A tentatively romantic
Figure once, she became
Merely an old lady like
Many another, with
Her favourite programme
And her sustaining faith.

She sits now and watches
Incredulously as some mad
Whippersnapper howls
His love-song and the gulls
Snuggle down on the beaches,
The rooks in the churchyard.

Old Roscoff

(*after Corbière*)

Bolt-hole of brigandage, old keep
Of piracy, the ocean booms
On membranes of your granite sleep
And thunders in your brackish dreams.
Snore the sea and snore the sky,
Snore the fog-horn in your ears;
Sleep with your one watchful eye
On England these three hundred years.

Sleep, old hulk for ever anchored
Where the wild goose and cormorant,
Your elegists, cry to the barred
And salt-laced shutters on the front.
Sleep, old whore of the homing seamen
Heady with wind and wine. No more
Will the hot gold subdue your women
As a spring tide engulfs your shore.

Sleep in the dunes beneath the grey
Gunmetal sky; the flags are gone.
No grape-shot now will ricochet
From spire and belfry. Pungent dawn
Will find your children dream-ensnared
By the great days when giants shook
The timbered piers and cynosured
The streets and market-place; but look —

Your cannon, swept by wintry rain,
Lie prostrate on their beds of mud.
Their mouths will never speak again;
They sleep the long sleep of the dead,
Their only roar the adenoidal
Echoes of equinoctial snores
From the cold muzzles pointing still
At England, trailing a few wild flowers.

Brecht in Svendborg

We have lashed oars on the thatch
To keep it down in everything
Short of a cyclone, and
The sun gilds our garden;
But deadly visions hang
Like rain-clouds in the sound.

A little boat with patched
Sails skates on the crinkly
Tinfoil of the bay; but we
Are not deceived by scenery.
Ears cocked, we can hear
Screams beyond the frontier.

The owl announces death
From the foliage these spring
Nights while I read *Macbeth*,
Kant, or the *Tao Tê Ching*;
Twice daily the starlings
Are silenced by a shriek

Of ordnance from the naval
War-games of the Reich.
The whitewash is peeling
From the damp ceiling
As I work at *Galileo*
In the converted stable.

Tacked to the oak beams,
A stage poster from
The old Schiffbauerdamm,
Faded now, proclaims
The truth is concrete.
Confucius' scroll portrait,

The ashtrays, cigar boxes
And drawers of microfilm
Make everything familiar.
From here I can watch
Helene gardening,
The children at the swing.

This could be home from home
If things were otherwise.
Twice daily the mails come
Up the sound in a ship;
I notice that the house
Has four doors for escape.

This poem is based on the English versions of *Svendborger Gedichte*
(1939) in Brecht's *Poems 1913-1956* (Eyre Methuen 1979).

Knut Hamsun in Old Age

While a late thaw began in the boarded eaves
I left, exhausted, that city nobody leaves
Without being marked by it; signed on
For Newcastle-upon-Tyne and so to Spain,
Renouncing the tightly corseted lives,
The many windows flashing in the sun.
Dream on, dream homes, until I come again!

Later the wives and the hard-earned estate,
The admiration of the acknowledged great;
But who could hope wholly to sublimate
The bad years, the imperious gratitude
Working like hunger at the very bone?
And so, my larder dim with surplus food,
My polished windows blazing in the sun,

Waking, these days, I sometimes think myself
Back in that attic with its empty shelf.
Strangely enough, it was enormous fun
Glaring, a madman, into the bun faces
Of outraged butchers and policemen
And acting the idiot in public places.
The conquering soul betrayed a manic grin.

Born of the earth, I made terms with the earth,
This being the only thing of lasting worth.
Beside my bed the dog-eared gods of art
Made way for fragrant works on crop rotation,
The agriculture where all cultures start.
The typewriter fell silent; rod and gun
Went out with me to prowl the watchful dawn.

Yes, I shook hands with Hitler; knew disgrace.
But time heals everything; I rose again.
Now I can look my butcher in the face.
Besides, did I not once, as a young man,
Cure myself of incipient tuberculosis
Inhaling four sub-zero nights and days
Perched on the screaming roof of a freight train?

One fortunate in both would have us choose
'Perfection of the life or of the work'.
Nonsense, you work best on a full stomach
As everybody over thirty knows —
For who, unbreakfasted, will love the lark?
Prepare your protein-fed epiphanies,
Your heavenly mansions blazing in the dark.

The Andean Flute

He dances to that music in the wood
As if history were no more than a dream.
Who said the banished gods were gone for good?

The furious rhythm creates a manic mood,
Piercing the twilight like a mountain stream.
He dances to that music in the wood.

We might have put on Bach or Buxtehude,
But a chance impulse chose the primal scream.
Who said the banished gods were gone for good?

An Inca frenzy fires his northern blood.
His child-heart picking up the tribal beam,
He dances to that music in the wood.

A puff of snow bursts where the birches brood;
Along the lane the earliest snowdrops gleam.
Who said the banished gods were gone for good?

It is the ancient cry for warmth and food
That moves him. Acting out an ancient theme,
He dances to that music in the wood.
Who said the banished gods were gone for good?

Tractatus

(*for Aidan Higgins*)

'The world is everything that is the case'
From the fly giving up in the coal-shed
To the Winged Victory of Samothrace.
Give blame, praise, to the fumbling God
Who hides, shame-facèdly, His agèd face;
Whose light retires behind its veil of cloud.

The world, though, is also so much more —
Everything that is the case imaginatively.
Tacitus believed mariners could *hear*
The sun sinking into the western sea;
And who would question that titanic roar,
The steam rising wherever the edge may be?

Katie at the Pool

My four-year-old daughter
points up at the low
ceiling with a cry:
'Look at the shadow
of the water on the sky!'

The Dawn Chorus

It is not sleep itself but dreams we miss,
Say the psychologists; and the poets too.
We yearn for that reality in this.

There is another world resides in this,
Said Éluard — not original, but true.
It is not sleep itself but dreams we miss.

If we could once achieve a synthesis
Of the archaic and the entirely new . . .
We yearn for that reality in this.

But, wide awake, clear-eyed with cowardice,
The flaming seraphim we find untrue.
It is not sleep itself but dreams we miss.

Listening heart-broken to the dawn chorus,
Clutching the certainty that once we flew,
We yearn for that reality in this.

Awaiting still our metamorphosis,
We hoard the fragments of what once we knew.
It is not sleep itself but dreams we miss.
We yearn for that reality in this.

Morning Radio

(*for John Scotney*)

The silence of the ether . . .
What can be going on
In the art-deco liner?

Ah, now the measured pips,
A stealth of strings
Tickling the fretwork throat,

Woodwinds entering
Delicately, the clarinet
Ascending to a lark-like note.

Seven o'clock —
News-time, and the merciful
Voice of Tom Crowe

Explains with sorrow
That the world we know
Is coming to an end.

Even as he speaks
We can hear furniture
Creak and slide on the decks.

But first a brief recital
Of resonant names —
Mozart, Schubert, Brahms.

The sun shines,
And a new day begins
To the strains of a horn concerto.

Table Talk

You think I am your servant but you are wrong —
The service lies with you. During your long
Labours at me, I am the indulgent wood,
Tolerant of your painstaking ineptitude.
Your poems were torn from me by violence;
I am here to receive your homage in dark silence.

Remembering the chain-saw surgery and the seaward groan,
Like a bound and goaded exodus from Babylon,
I pray for a wood-spirit to make me dance,
To scare your pants off and upset your balance,
Destroy the sedate poise with which you pour
Forth your ephemeral stream of literature.

When I was a pine and lived in a cold climate
I listened to leaf-rumours about our fate;
But I have come a long way since then
To watch the sun glint on your reflective pen.
The hurt I do resent, and my consolation
Will be the unspoilt paper when you have gone.

And yet I love you, even in your ignorance,
Perhaps because at last you are making sense —
Talking to me, not through me, recognizing
That it is I alone who let you sing
Wood music. Hitherto shadowy and dumb,
I speak to you now as your indispensable medium.

Another Sunday Morning

We wake and watch the sun make bright
The corners of our London flat —
No sound but the sporadic, surly
Snarl of a car making an early
Dash for the country or the coast.
This is the time I like the most
When, for an hour or two, the strife
And strain of the late bourgeois life

Let up, we lie and grin to hear
The children bickering next door —
Hilarious formulations based
On a weird logic we have lost.
Oil crises and vociferous crowds
Seem as far off as tiny clouds;
The long-range forecast prophesies
Mean temperatures and azure skies.

Out in the park where Celia's father
Died, the Sunday people gather —
Residents towed by Afghan hounds,
Rastafarians trailing 'sounds',
Provincial tourists, Japanese
Economists, Saudi families,
Fresh-faced American college kids
Making out in the green shades.

A chiliastic prig, I prowl
Among the dog-lovers and growl,
Among the kite-fliers and fly
The private kite of poetry —
A sort of winged sandwich board
El-Grecoed to receive the Lord;
An airborne, tremulous brochure
Proclaiming that the end is near.

Black diplomats with stately wives,
Sauntering by, observe the natives
Dozing beside the palace gates —
Old ladies under wide straw-hats
Who can remember *Chu Chin Chow*
And Kitchener. Exhausted now
By decades of retrenchment, they
Wait for the rain at close of play.

So many empires come and gone —
The spear and scimitar laid down,
The long-bow and the arquebus
Adapted to domestic use.
A glimpse of George V at Cowes
Lives on behind the wrinkled brows
Of an old man in Bognor Regis
Making dreadnoughts out of matches.

Asia now for a thousand years —
A flower that blooms and disappears
In a sand-storm; every artifact
A pure, self-referential act,
That the intolerant soul may be
Retrieved from triviality
And the locked heart, so long in pawn
To steel, redeemed by wood and stone.

A Lighthouse in Maine

It might be anywhere,
That ivory tower
Approached by a dirt road.

Bleached stone against
Bleached sky, it faces
Every way with an air

Of squat omniscience —
A polished Buddha
Hard and bright beyond

Vegetable encroachment.
The north light
That strikes its frame

Houses is not
The light of heaven
But that of this world;

Nor is its task
To throw a punctual
Glow in the dark

To liners wild
With rock music and calm
With navigation.

Though built to shed
Light, it prefers
To shelter it, as it does

Now in the one-bird hour
Of afternoon, a milky
Glare melting the telephone poles.

It works both ways,
Of course, light
Being, like love and the cold,

Something that you
Can give and keep
At the same time.

Night and day it sits
Above the ocean like
A kindly eye, keeping

And giving the rainbow
Of its many colours,
Each of them white.

It might be anywhere —
Hokkaido, Mayo, Maine;
But it is in Maine.

You make a right
Somewhere beyond Rockland,
A left, a right,

You turn a corner and
There it is, shining
In modest glory like

The soul of Adonais.
Out you get and
Walk the rest of the way.

St. Eustace

The hunt ceases
Here; there will be no more
Deranged pursuit of the mild-eyed
Creatures of the countryside.
   Startled, he reins before
   His nemesis

   And stares amazed
   At the hanged man of wood —
Gawain caught in the cold cathedral
Light of a temperate forest, Paul
   Blind on a desert road,
   One hand upraised.

   He will not burn,
   Now, with such nonchalance
Agape beasts to the gods of Rome
Whose strident, bronze imperium
   He served devoutly once
   But in his turn

   Rotate above
   A charcoal brazier,
Braised in his own fat for his contumacy
And vision; in his dying briefly
   One with the hind, the hare
   And the ring-dove.

144

The Joycentenary Ode

Aged twenty-odd, I spent
A night straitched
Between blankets on

The cold floor
Of your squat tower,
Gymsoul, my ho head heavy

As yonder stone among
Half-empty rosbif
And electricity glasses.

There I dreamed
The wholething from
Once upon a time

To riverrun, from
Creak of dawn
To crack of doom,

And woke to find
The scrotum-tightening glittering
Like razor-blades.

What can I tell you,
Jerms, where you straitch
In the Flutherin Symatery?

What pome of mine might
Healp aliviate
Youretournal night?

What news of the warld
You loft bihand
Widdamuse you now?

The goodguise bate
The badgoys in
Diturrible fright

That drove you from
Parease to die
In switzocclusion.

And now we have
Emergency fones in coffins
As you proposed.

Everbaddy reads
Your wooks now in
Unlimited eruditions;

And if you niverwan
The Noble Praise,
Well, that reflects upon

Our precontraceptions
About lutherature and erges
Your origeniosity.

Gemsbounder has replaced
Hopalongcarcity
At the Pavlodeograph;

The pap democrisy
You realised has become
Thanew art forrum.

Spundrawers in every
Kirtschen! Airwickers
In ivery bahrfrheum!

A noddindog in the rear
Winda of avery carr!
A bonne in overy hoven!

The bairdboard
Bombardment screen
And gineral californucation

Have revolationized
Ourland beyand raggednition.
Nialson came down

A tunderish clap,
Aye-eye in the dust;
And soon there will be

A new ring-roarrrd built
On reclaimed land
Offa manies a strand.

But some things change
So slowly they
Are still there when

Time comes round again,
Like the dark rain
Muttering on the grave

Of the consumptive
Boy from the gas-works
Who died for love.

Gazing wist, folden
Gavriels, aingles of leidt,
We cmome to a place

Beyond cumminity
Where only the wind synges.
Words faoil there

Bifar infunity,
One evenereal stare
Twintwinkling on the sea.

This is the dark aidge
Where the souil swails
With hurtfealt soang,

Hearing the sonerous
Volapuke of the waives,
That ainchant tongue,

Dialect of what thribe,
Throb of what broken heart —
A language beyond art

That not even you,
If you lived
To a hunderd and wan,
Could begin to danscribe.

A Postcard from Berlin

(for Paul Durcan)

We know the cities by their stones
Where Ararat flood-water shines
And violets have struggled through
The bloody dust. Skies are the blue
Of postcard skies, and the leaves green
In that quaint quarter of Berlin.
Wool-gatheringly, the clouds migrate:
No checkpoint checks their tenuous flight.

I hear echoes of Weimar tunes,
Grosz laughter in the beer-gardens
Of a razed Reich, and rumbling tyres
Unter den Linden; but the fires
Of abstract rage, exhausted there,
Blaze out of control elsewhere —
Perhaps one reason you pursue
This night-hunt with no end in view.

I can imagine your dismay
As, cornered in some zinc café,
You read of another hunger-strike,
A postman blasted off his bike . . .
Oh, Hölderlin no fly would hurt,
Our vagabond and pilgrim spirit,
Give us a ring on your way back
And tell us what the nations lack!

One of these Nights

A pregnant moon of August
Composes the roof-tops'
Unventilated slopes;
Dispenses to the dust
Its milky balm. A blue
Buzzard blinks in the zoo.

Cashel and Angkor Wat
Are not more ghostly than
London now, its squares
Bone-pale in the moonlight,
Its quiet thoroughfares
A map of desolation.

The grime of an ephemeral
Culture is swept clean
By that celestial hoover,
The refuse of an era
Consumed like cellophane
In its impartial glare.

A train trembles deep
In the earth; vagrants sleep
Beside the revolving doors
Of vast department stores
Past whose alarm systems
The moonlight blandly streams.

A breeze-ruffled news-stand
Headlines the dole queues,
The bleak no-longer-news
Of racism and inflation —
Straws in the rising wind
That heralds the cyclone.

It all happened before —
The road to Wigan Pier,
The long road from Jarrow
To the tea-room at the Ritz;
Munich, the Phony War,
The convoys and the Blitz.

One of these nights quiescent
Sirens will start to go
— A dog-howl reminiscent
Of forty years ago —
And sleepy people file
Down to the shelters while

Radiant warplanes come
Droning up the Thames from
Gravesend to Blackfriars,
Westminster and Mayfair,
Their incandescent flowers
Unfolding everywhere.

Next time will be the last
But, safe in the underground
With tea and *Picture Post*,
We'll take out the guitar
And pass the gaspers round
The way we did before;
And life will begin once more.

A Garage in Co. Cork

Surely you paused at this roadside oasis
In your nomadic youth, and saw the mound
Of never-used cement, the curious faces,
The soft-drink ads and the uneven ground
Rainbowed with oily puddles, where a snail
Had scrawled its slimy, phosphorescent trail.

Like a frontier store-front in an old western
It might have nothing behind it but thin air,
Building materials, fruit boxes, scrap iron,
Dust-laden shrubs and coils of rusty wire,
A cabbage white fluttering in the sodden
Silence of an untended kitchen garden —

Nirvana! But the cracked panes reveal a dark
Interior echoing with the cries of children.
Here in this quiet corner of Co. Cork
A family ate, slept, and watched the rain
Dance clean and cobalt the exhausted grit
So that the mind shrank from the glare of it.

Where did they go? South Boston? Cricklewood?
Somebody somewhere thinks of this as home,
Remembering the old pumps where they stood,
Antique now, squirting juice into a chrome
Lagonda or a dung-caked tractor while
A cloud swam on a cloud-reflecting tile.

Surely a whitewashed sun-trap at the back
Gave way to hens, wild thyme, and the first few
Shadowy yards of an overgrown cart track,
Tyres in the branches such as Noah knew —
Beyond, a swoop of mountain where you heard,
Disconsolate in the haze, a single blackbird.

Left to itself, the functional will cast
A death-bed glow of picturesque abandon.
The intact antiquities of the recent past,
Dropped from the retail catalogues, return
To the materials that gave rise to them
And shine with a late sacramental gleam.

A god who spent the night here once rewarded
Natural courtesy with eternal life —
Changing to petrol pumps, that they be spared
For ever there, an old man and his wife.
The virgin who escaped his dark design
Sanctions the townland from her prickly shrine.

We might be anywhere but are in one place only,
One of the milestones of earth-residence
Unique in each particular, the thinly
Peopled hinterland serenely tense —
Not in the hope of a resplendent future
But with a sure sense of its intrinsic nature.

The Woods

Two years we spent
down there, in a quaint
outbuilding bright with recent paint.

A green retreat,
secluded and sedate,
part of a once great estate,

it watched our old
bone-shaker as it growled
with guests and groceries through heat and cold,

and heard you tocsin
meal-times with a spoon
while I sat working in the sun.

Above the yard
an old clock had expired
the night Lenin arrived in Petrograd.

Hapsburgs and Romanovs
had removed their gloves
in the drawing-rooms and alcoves

of the manor house;
but these illustrious
ghosts never imposed on us.

Enough that the pond
steamed, the apples ripened,
the chestnuts on the gravel opened.

Ragwort and hemlock,
cinquefoil and ladysmock
throve in the shadows at the back;

beneath the trees
foxgloves and wood-anemones
looked up with tearful metamorphic eyes.

We woke the rooks
on narrow, winding walks
familiar from the story-books,

or visited
a disused garden shed
where gas-masks from the war decayed;

and we knew peace
splintering the thin ice
on the bathtub drinking-trough for cows.

But how could we
survive indefinitely
so far from the city and the sea?

Finding, at last,
too creamy for our taste
the fat profusion of that feast,

we carried on
to chaos and confusion,
our birthright and our proper portion.

Another light
than ours convenes the mute
attention of those woods tonight —

while we, released
from that pale paradise,
confront the darkness in another place.

Craigvara House

That was the year
of the black nights and clear
mornings, a mild elation touched with fear;

a watchful anomie,
heart silence, day-long reverie
while the wind made harp-strings on the sea

and the first
rain of winter burst
earthwards as if quenching a great thirst.

A mist of spray
hung over the shore all day
while I slumped there re-reading *La Nausée*

or watched a cup
turn mantra on a table-top
like Scott Fitzgerald after the crack-up;

or knocked a coal,
releasing squeaky gas until
it broke and tumbled into its hot hole.

Night fell on a rough
sea, on a moonlit basalt cliff,
huts with commandments painted on the roof,

and rain wept down
the raw slates of the town,
cackling maniacally in pipe and drain.

I slowly came
to treasure my ashram
(a flat with a sea view, the living room

furnished with frayed
chintz, cane chairs and faded
water-colours of Slemish and Fair Head —

no phone, no television,
nothing to break my concentration,
the new-won knowledge of my situation;

and it was there,
choosing my words with care,
I sat down and began to write once more.

When snowflakes
wandered on to the rocks
I thought, home is where the heart breaks —

the lost domain
of week-ends in the rain,
the Sunday sundae and the sexual pain.

I stared each night
at a glow of yellow light
over the water where the interned sat tight

(I in my own prison
envying their fierce reason,
their solidarity and extroversion)

and during storms
imagined the clenched farms
with dreadful faces thronged and fiery arms.

Sometime before
spring I found in there
the frequency I had been looking for

and crossed by night
a dark channel, my eyesight
focused upon a flickering pier-light.

I slept then and,
waking early, listened
entranced to the pea-whistle sound

of a first thrush
practising on a thorn bush
a new air picked up in Marrakesh.

And then your car
parked with a known roar
and you stood smiling at the door —

as if we might
consider a bad night
as over and step out into the sunlight.

The Terminal Bar

(*for Philip Haas*)

The television set hung
in its wire-net cage,
protected from the flung
bottles of casual rage,
is fetish and icon
providing all we want
of magic and redemption,
routine and sentiment.
The year-old tinsels hang
where an unclaimed no-hoper
trembles; fly-corpses cling
to the grimy fly-paper.
Manhattan snows swarm
on constellated waters,
steam trails from warm
subway ventilators . . .
Welcome to the planet,
its fluorescent beers
buzzing in the desolate
silence of the spheres.
Slam the door and knock
the snow from your shoe,
admit that the vast dark
at last defeated you.
Nobody found the Grail
or conquered outer space;
join the clientele
watching itself increase.

After Pasternak

1. *White Night*
In the distant past I can see
A house on a Moscow quay,
Your first flat, where you,
A daughter of the steppe,
Had come from Kursk to be
A student and fall in love.

One white night we sat late
At your window, gazing out
At the city stretching away
Beyond the oil-dark Volga,
Gas-flames flickering
Like moths in the street-lamps.

That spring-white night we spoke
Tentatively, constrained
By mysteries while, far off
In the countryside, nightingales
Thronged the thick forests
With the thunder of their song.

The singing went on and on,
The birds' tiny voices
Echoing like a choir
Deep in enchanted woods;
And there the dawn wind bore
The sound of our own words.

Fruit-trees were in flower
As far as the eye could reach,
And ghostly birches crowded
Into the roads as though
To wave goodbye to the white
Night which had seen so much.

2. *The Earth*
Spring bursts in the houses
Of Moscow; a moth quits
Its hiding place and flits
Into the light of day
To gasp on cotton blouses;
Fur coats are locked away.

The aspidistra shakes itself
And stretches in its pot;
Attic and dusty shelf
Inhale the open air.
This is the time for twilit
Trysts beside the river,

Time for the injudicious
Out-in-the-open voices
And gossip like thaw-water
Dripping from the eaves.
Sob stories and laughter
Dance in the woken leaves.

Outside and in, the same
Mixture of fire and fear,
The same delirium
Of apple-blossom at
Window and garden gate,
Tram stop and factory door.

So why does the dim horizon
Weep, and the dark mould
Resist? It is my chosen
Task, surely, to nurse
The distances from cold,
The earth from loneliness.

Which is why, in the spring,
Our friends come together
And the vodka and talking
Are ceremonies, that the river
Of suffering may release
The heart-constraining ice.

The Globe in North Carolina

There are no religions, no revelations;
  there are women.
                    — Voznesensky, *Antiworlds*

The earth spins to my finger-tips and
Pauses beneath my outstretched hand;
White water seethes against the green
Capes where the continents begin.
Warm breezes move the pines and stir
The hot dust of the piedmont where
Night glides inland from town to town.
I love to see that sun go down.

It sets in a coniferous haze
Beyond Tennessee; the anglepoise
Rears like a moon to shed its savage
Radiance on the desolate page,
On Dvořàk sleeves and Audubon
Bird-prints. An electronic brain
Records the concrete music of
Our hardware in the heavens above.

From Hatteras to the Blue Ridge
Night spreads like ink on the unhedged
Tobacco fields and clucking lakes,
Bringing the lights on in the rocks
And swamps, the farms and motor courts,
Substantial cities, kitsch resorts —
Until, to the mild theoptic eye,
America is its own night-sky,

Its own celestial fruit, on which
Sidereal forms appear, their rich
Clusters and vague attenuations
Miming galactic dispositions.

Hesperus is a lighthouse, Mars
An air-force base; molecular cars
Arrowing the turnpikes become
Lost meteorites in search of home.

No doubt we could go on like this
For decades yet; but nemesis
Awaits our furious make-believe,
Our harsh refusal to conceive
A world so different from our own
We wouldn't know it were we shown.
Who, in its halcyon days, imagined
Carthage a ballroom for the wind?

And what will the new night be like?
Why, as before, a partial dark
Stage-lit by a mysterious glow
As in the *Night Hunt* of Uccello.
Era-provincial self-regard
Finds us, as ever, unprepared
For the odd shifts of emphasis
Time regularly throws up to us.

Here, as elsewhere, I recognize
A wood invisible for its trees
Where everything must change except
The fact of change; our scepticism
And irony, grown trite, be dumb
Before the new thing that must come
Out of the scrunched Budweiser can
To make us sadder, wiser men.

Out in the void and staring hard
At the dim stone where we were reared,
Great mother, now the gods have gone
We place our faith in you alone,
Inverting the procedures which
Knelt us to things beyond our reach.
Drop of the ocean, may your salt
Astringency redeem our fault!

Veined marble, if we only knew,
In practice as in theory, true
Redemption lies not in the thrust
Of action only, but the trust
We place in our peripheral
Night garden in the glory-hole
Of space, a home from home, and what
Devotion we can bring to it!

. . . You lie, an ocean to the east,
Your limbs composed, your mind at rest,
Asleep in a sunrise which will be
Your mid-day when it reaches me;
And what misgivings I might have
About the true importance of
The 'merely human' pale before
The mere fact of your being there.

Five miles away a south-bound freight
Sings its euphoria to the state
And passes on; unfinished work
Awaits me in the scented dark.
The halved globe, slowly turning, hugs
Its silence, while the lightning bugs
Are quiet beneath the open window,
Listening to that lonesome whistle blow . . .

Squince

The eyes are clouded where
  He lies in a veined dish.
Is this the salmon of wisdom
  Or merely a dead fish?

A forest of symbols here —
  Swan, heron, goat,
Druidic stone circle, fuchsia-
  Buried hill-fort;

And the village is of clear-cut
  Resonant artifacts:
A pink-washed grocery shop,
  A yellow *telefón* box.

We live now in a future
  Prehistory, the ancient
Mystery surviving in
  The power to enchant

Of the sun going down
  In a thicket of hazel trees
While ferns at the window
  Nod in the everbreeze.

Mt. Gabriel

As if planted there by giant golfers in the skies,
White in the gloaming, last before New Brunswick,
The geodesic domes have left their caves
To sit out in the summer sunset. Angels
Beamed at Namancos and Bayona, sick
With exile, they yearn homeward now, their eyes
Tuned to the ultramarine, first-star-pierced dark
Reflected on the dark, incoming waves —
Who, aliens, burnt-out meteorites, time capsules,
Are here for ever now as intermediaries
Between the big bang and our scattered souls.

Tithonus

. . . and after the fire a still small voice.
                              1 *Kings*, xix, 12

Worm will see the light in a desert.
                    — Beckett, *The Unnamable*

The irony here
Is that I survive
While the gods

Who so decreed,
And so many more,
Are long since dead.

It is cold, dark,
And I am alone
On this rolling stone —

Awaiting, as I have done
For centuries,
My transfiguration,

Nattering on
As my habit is,
God knows why:

An impulse merely,
Perhaps, to break
The unquiet silence.

Whenever I stop
There is only the wind.
There used to be

Other crickets
Like me, dry sticks
Straining their lights.

No lights now, not
A cheep out of them
Who shone so valiantly.

Nature loves to hide,
Heraclitus said,
But nature is dead:

There are no branches
To frame the eyes
Of my contemporaries.

I hoped to catch
My death, to croak
On this mountainside;

But Eos' wish
Proved greater
Than any winter.

I forget nothing
But if I told
Everything in detail —

Not merely Golgotha
And Krakatoa
But the leaf-plink

Of rain-drops after
Thermopylae,
The lizard-flick

In the scrub as Genghis
Khan entered Peking
And the changing clouds,

I would need
Another eternity,
Perish the thought.

I dream of the past,
Of the future,
Even of the present.

Perhaps I am really
Dead and dreaming
My vigilance?

'Gleaming halls
Of morn', my eye:
The sun will rise

On cinders, ashes,
Their textures bright
By nuclear light,

No Dresden angel
Or Hiroshima bas-relief
To sanctify the ruins

But a violent
Riot of wild flowers
Splitting the rocks.

There used to be cars
From time to time
When this was Ethiopia.

I would blaze and shout
As they rumbled past
In a cloud of dust

But they never stopped;
And after a while
I would scratch

And watch the sky,
The sun on stone,
Night coming on.

Who do I know?
There was one, Echo,
Who came to grief

In similar fashion —
A voice, her bones
Restored to stones.

The only one I
Envy is Endymion
Whom Selene fixed up

With eternal youth
And placed in a coma
To obviate insomnia.

There she is now,
Her faint light
Shining on everything.

Like her I am
A shadow
Of my former self.

If they could see
Me now, reduced
To this absurdity . . .

Perhaps I shall die
At long last,
Face in the dust —

Having seen,
Not that I asked,
The light in the desert.

Girls on the Bridge

— Pykene na Brukken, Munch, 1900

Audible trout,
Notional midges. Beds,
Lamplight and crisp linen wait
In the house there for the sedate
Limbs and averted heads
Of the girls out

Late on the bridge.
The dusty road that slopes
Past is perhaps the high road south,
A symbol of world-wondering youth,
Of adolescent hopes
And privileges;

But stops to find
The girls content to gaze
At the unplumbed, reflective lake,
Their plangent conversational quack
Expressive of calm days
And peace of mind.

Grave daughters
Of time, you lightly toss
Your hair as the long shadows grow
And night begins to fall. Although
Your laughter calls across
The dark waters,

A ghastly sun
Watches in pale dismay.
Oh, you may laugh, being as you are
Fair sisters of the evening star,
But wait — if not today
A day will dawn

When the bad dreams
You scarcely know will scatter
The punctual increment of your lives.
The road resumes, and where it curves,
A mile from where you chatter,
Somebody screams.

The girls are dead,
The house and pond have gone.
Steel bridge and concrete highway gleam
And sing in the arctic dark; the scream
We started at is grown
The serenade

Of an insane
And monstrous age. We live
These days as on a different planet,
One without trout or midges on it,
Under the arc-lights of
A mineral heaven;

And we have come,
Despite ourselves, to no
True notion of our proper work,
But wander in the dazzling dark
Amid the drifting snow
Dreaming of some

Lost evening when
Our grandmothers, if grand
Mothers we had, stood at the edge
Of womanhood on a country bridge
And gazed at a still pond
And knew no pain.

The Hunt by Night

— Uccello, 1465

Flickering shades,
Stick figures, lithe game,
Swift flights of bison in a cave
Where man the maker killed to live;
But neolithic bush became
The midnight woods

Of nursery walls,
The ancient fears mutated
To play, horses to rocking-horses
Tamed and framed to courtly uses,
Crazed no more by foetid
Bestial howls

But rampant to
The pageantry they share
And echoes of the hunting horn
At once peremptory and forlorn.
The mild herbaceous air
Is lemon-blue,

The glade aglow
With pleasant mysteries,
Diuretic depots, pungent prey;
And midnight hints at break of day
Where, among sombre trees,
The slim dogs go

Wild with suspense
Leaping to left and right,
Their cries receding to a point
Masked by obscurities of paint —
As if our hunt by night,
So very tense,

So long pursued,
In what dark cave begun
And not yet done, were not the great
Adventure we suppose but some elaborate
Spectacle put on for fun
And not for food.

Brighton Beach

(for Paul Smyth)

1.
Remember those awful parties
In dreary Belfast flats,
The rough sectarian banter
In Lavery's back bar,
The boisterous take-aways
And moonlight on wet slates?

Remember the place you rented
At the end of a muddy lane
Somewhere near Muckamore?
No light, so in midwinter
You slept in the afternoon
And lay there until dawn.

Remember the time we drove
To Donegal and you talked
For hours to fishermen
You had worked with while I,
Out of my depths in those
Waters, loafed on the quays?

Now, pushing forty, we roam
At ease along the prom,
Life-buffeted to be sure
But grown sober and wise.
The sea shuffles ashore
Beneath pale mackerel skies.

2.
From the far end of the pier
I imagine the sun-gleam
On a thousand *deux-chevaux*.
Over there they explore
Balbec and sip Pernod
In a Monet-monoxide dream.

Europe thrives, but the off-shore
Islanders year by year
Decline, the spirit of empire
Fugitive as always.
Now, in this rancorous peace,
Should come the spirit of place.

Too late though, for already
Places as such are dead
Or nearly; the loved sea
Reflects banality.
Not so in the old days
The retired sailor says.

But the faded Georgian bricks
Towering over the shore
Remain, like the upright
Old men with walking-sticks
Out for a last stroll before
Turning in for the night.

Achill

im chaonaí uaigneach nach mór go bhfeicim an lá

I lie and imagine a first light gleam in the bay
    After one more night of erosion and nearer the grave,
Then stand and gaze from the window at break of day
    As a shearwater skims the ridge of an incoming wave;
And I think of my son a dolphin in the Aegean,
    A sprite among sails knife-bright in a seasonal wind,
And wish he were here where currachs walk on the ocean
    To ease with his talk the solitude locked in my mind.

I sit on a stone after lunch and consider the glow
    Of the sun through mist, a pearl bulb containèdly fierce;
A rain-shower darkens the schist for a minute or so
    Then it drifts away and the sloe-black patches disperse.
Croagh Patrick towers like Naxos over the water
    And I think of my daughter at work on her difficult art
And wish she were with me now between thrush and plover,
    Wild thyme and sea-thrift, to lift the weight from my heart.

The young sit smoking and laughing on the bridge at evening
    Like birds on a telephone pole or notes on a score.
A tin whistle squeals in the parlour, once more it is raining,
    Turf-smoke inclines and a wind whines under the door;
And I lie and imagine the lights going on in the harbour
    Of white-housed Náousa, your clear definition at night,
And wish you were here to upstage my disconsolate labour
    As I glance through a few thin pages and switch off the light.

Ovid in Tomis

What coarse god
Was the gear-box in the rain
Beside the road?

What nereid the unsinkable
Coca-Cola
Knocking the icy rocks?

They stare me out
With the chaste gravity
And feral pride

Of noble savages
Set down
On an alien shore.

It is so long
Since my own transformation
Into a stone,

I often forget
That there was a time
Before my name

Was mud in the mouths
Of the Danube,
A dirty word in Rome.

Imagine Byron banished
To Botany Bay
Or Wilde to Dawson City

And you have some idea
How it is for me
On the shores of the Black Sea.

I who once strode
Head-high in the forum,
A living legend,

Fasten my sheepskin
By greasy waters
In a Scythian wind.

My wife and friends
Do what they can
On my behalf;

Though from Tiberius,
Whom God preserve,
I expect nothing.

But I don't want
To die here
In the back of beyond

Among these morose
Dice-throwing Getes
And the dust of Thrace.

No doubt, in time
To come, this huddle of
Mud huts will be

A handsome city,
An important port,
A popular resort,

With an oil pipeline,
Martini terraces
And even a dignified

Statue of *me*
Gazing out to sea
From the promenade;

But for the moment
It is merely a place
Where I have to be.

Six years now
Since my relegation
To this 'town'

By the late Augustus.
The *Halieutica*,
However desultory,

Gives me a sense
Of purpose,
However factitious;

But I think it's the birds
That please me most,
The cranes and pelicans.

I often sit in the dunes
Listening hard
To the uninhibited

Virtuosity of a lark
Serenading the sun
And meditate upon

The transience
Of earthly dominion,
The perfidy of princes.

Mediocrity, they say,
Consoles itself
With the reflection

That genius so often
Comes to a bad end.
The things adversity

Teaches us
About human nature
As the aphorisms strike home!

I know the simple life
Would be right for me
If I were a simple man.

I have a real sense
Of the dumb spirit
In boulder and tree;

Skimming stones, I wince
With vicarious pain
As a slim quoit goes in.

And the six-foot reeds
Of the delta,
The pathos there!

Whenever they bend
And sigh in the wind
It is not merely Syrinx

Remembering Syrinx
But Syrinx keening
Her naked terror

Of the certain future,
She and her kind
Being bulk-destined

For the pulping machines
And the cording
Of motor-car tyres.

Pan is dead, and already
I feel an ancient
Unity leave the earth,

The bowl avoid my eye
As if ashamed
Of my failure to keep faith.

(It knows that I
Have exchanged belief
For documentation.)

The Muse is somewhere
Else, not here
By this frozen lake —

Or, if here, then I am
Not poet enough
To make the connection.

Are we truly alone
With our physics and myths,
The stars no more

Than glittering dust,
With no-one there
To hear our choral odes?

If so, we can start
To ignore the silence
Of the infinite spaces

And concentrate instead
On the infinity
Under our very noses —

The cry at the heart
Of the artichoke,
The gaiety of atoms.

Better to contemplate
The blank page
And leave it blank

Than modify
Its substance by
So much as a pen-stroke.

Woven of wood-nymphs,
It speaks volumes
No-one will ever write.

I incline my head
To its candour
And weep for our exile.

October in Hyde Park

The white-washed monastery where we sat
listening to the Aegean and watched
a space capsule among the stars
will be closed now for the winter;
and the harbour bars,
cleared of the yacht crowd,
will be serving dawn ouzos to the crews
of the *Aghios Ioannis* and *Nikolaos*
where they play dominoes
by the light of a paraffin lamp.

Europe, after the first rain of winter,
shines with a corpse-light.
A cold wind scours the condemned playground;
leaves swarm like dead souls
down bleak avenues as if they led
to the kingdoms of the dead.
An alcoholic defector
picks out 'Rock of Ages' with one finger
on the grand piano in his Moscow flat,
his long day's journey into night
almost complete. Some cold fate
awaits us at the ends of the earth.

Like the leaves we are coming within
sight of the final river,
its *son et lumière*
and breath of the night sea.
As if ghosts already,
we search our pockets for the Stygian fare.

Dejection

Bone-idle, I lie listening to the rain,
Not tragic now nor yet to frenzy bold.
Must I stand out in thunder-storms again
Who have twice come in from the cold?

Night Drive

— St. Petersburg, 1900

(*after Rilke*)

Not drawn but flown by glistening mares
past silent, tomb-lit porticoes
and lamp-posts hung like chandeliers,
past granite palaces where a first
dawn-glow lightened the roofs, we burst
on to the windy Neva quays,
rumbling there in an anxious, thin
half-light neither of earth nor heaven,
leaving behind the unwoken, dark
woods of the Czar's private park
protected from the risen breeze,
its statues fading, every gest-
ure frozen for ever in the past.
St. Petersburg ceased to exist,
disclosed that it had never been;
asked only peace now, as if one
long mad should find the knot untied
and watch, recovered and clear-eyed,
a fixed idea in its Byzantine,
varnished and adamantine shrine
spin off from the whirling mind
and vanish, leaving not a trace behind.

Antarctica

(for Richard Ryan)

'I am just going outside and may be some time.'
The others nod, pretending not to know.
At the heart of the ridiculous, the sublime.

He leaves them reading and begins to climb,
Goading his ghost into the howling snow;
He is just going outside and may be some time.

The tent recedes beneath its crust of rime
And frostbite is replaced by vertigo:
At the heart of the ridiculous, the sublime.

Need we consider it some sort of crime,
This numb self-sacrifice of the weakest? No,
He is just going outside and may be some time —

In fact, for ever. Solitary enzyme,
Though the night yield no glimmer there will glow,
At the heart of the ridiculous, the sublime.

He takes leave of the earthly pantomime
Quietly, knowing it is time to go.
'I am just going outside and may be some time.'
At the heart of the ridiculous, the sublime.

Kinsale

The kind of rain we knew is a thing of the past —
deep-delving, dark, deliberate you would say,
browsing on spire and bogland; but today
our sky-blue slates are steaming in the sun,
our yachts tinkling and dancing in the bay
like race-horses. We contemplate at last
shining windows, a future forbidden to no-one.

Death and the Sun

(Albert Camus, 1913-1960)

Le soleil ni la mort ne se peuvent regarder fixement.

When the car spun from the road and your neck broke
I was hearing rain on the school bicycle shed
Or tracing the squeaky enumerations of chalk;
And later, while you lay in the *mairie*,
I pedalled home from Bab-el-Oued
To my mother silently making tea,
Bent to my homework in the firelight
Or watched an old film on television —
Gunfights under a blinding desert sun,
Bogartian urgencies in the cold Ulster night.

How we read you then, admiring the frank composure
Of a stranger bayed by dogs who could not hear
The interior dialogue of flesh and stone,
His life and death a work of art
Conceived in the silence of the heart.
Not that he would ever have said so, no,
He would merely have taken a rush-hour tram
To a hot beach white as a scream,
Stripped to a figure of skin and bone
And struck out, a back-stroke, as far as he could go.

Deprived though we were of his climatic privileges
And raised in a northern land of rain and muck,
We too knew the familiar foe, the blaze
Of headlights on a coast road, the cicadas
Chattering like watches in our sodden hedges;
Yet never imagined the plague to come,
So long had it crouched there in the dark —
The *cordon sanitaire*, the stricken home,

Rats on the pavement, rats in the mind,
'St. James Infirmary' playing to the plague wind.

'An edifying abundance of funeral parlours',
The dead on holiday, cloth caps and curlers,
The shoe-shine and the thrice-combed wave
On Sunday morning and Saturday night;
Wee shadows fighting in a smoky cave
Who would one day be brought to light —
The modes of pain and pleasure,
These were the things to treasure
When times changed and your kind broke camp.
Diogenes in the dog-house, you carried a paraffin lamp.

Meanwhile in the night of Europe, the winter of faces,
Sex and opinion, a deft hand removes
The Just Judges from their rightful places
And hangs them behind a bar in Amsterdam —
A desert of fog and water, a cloudy dream
Where an antique Indonesian god grimaces
And relativity dawns like a host of doves;
Where the artist who refused suicide
Trades solidarity for solitude,
A night watch, a self-portrait, supper at Emmaus.

The lights are going on in towns that no longer exist.
Night falls on Belfast, on the just and the unjust,
On its Augustinian austerities of sand and stone —
While Sisyphus' descendants, briefly content,
Stand in the dole queues and roll their own.
Malraux described these preterite to you
As no longer historically significant;
And certainly they are shrouded in white dust.
All souls leprous, blinded by truth, each ghost
Steams on the shore as if awaiting rescue.

One cannot look for long at death or the sun.
Imagine Plato's neolithic troglodyte
Released from his dark cinema, released even
From the fire proper, so that he stands at last,
Absurd and anxious, out in the open air
And gazes, shading his eyes, at the world there —
Tangible fact ablaze in a clear light
That casts no shadow, where the vast
Sun gongs its lenity from a brazen heaven
Listening in silence to his rich despair.